Possessed Dogs Might Bite

Cover design by Veronica Rocha
Interior design by Veronica Rocha
Edited by Sydney Rain

ISBN:978-0-6455830-4-5
First edition

*To the ones who made it harder—
and to the one who kept going: me.
Special thanks to Memento, a friend, for
reading the first draft*

CHAPTER 1

The ice moon hung low over the ocean, casting a silver glow on the restless waves of Venus's shallow seas. Zel's small figure cut through the water, her determined strokes propelling her toward the floating heap. The knife clamped between her teeth gleamed in the night. She shouldn't be doing it. At all. Zel might have been right in spirit, but was wrong in everything else. A few of her wrongs:

She was attempting it alone. Despite being a confident swimmer, and in shallow water, she really should have someone with her.

And Zel was swimming at night.

Beneath the surface, the underwater world brimmed with life. Zel's heart pounded with anxiety and urgency as she got closer to the ghost net—an all-white sea turtle tangled within it. Its huge, pale, shimmering shell stood out against the dark water. It looked exhausted, barely holding on. It wasn't even able to stay above the water. Zel swam faster.

Meanwhile, onshore, Zel's mother, followed by a green schnauzer, paced on the soft sand, the beam of her flashlight sweeping the beach. "Zel! Where are you?" she called.

Zel dove and couldn't hear her mother's cries. She focused on the creature. The turtle's red eyes met hers, and she felt a connection—a silent plea for help. Zel took the knife and made quick work of the net across the turtle's shell. She was a little afraid it would bite her fingers off with its sharp beak. But when Zel freed the last strand of net, the turtle swam in a circle around her, as if in gratitude. Then Zel noticed a very deep wound on its neck, with a strand of the net still wrapped around it.

Breaking the surface, Zel gasped for air, her cheeks flushed from the cold. She grinned, and happiness flooded her for freeing it, but she still needed to take it to shore. She dove again.

On the beach, Mom sighed in relief when Zel emerged from the waves. Zel held a white turtle and a ghost net.

Mom rushed to her daughter, her voice a mix of scolding and concern. "What were you thinking?"

Zel panted and shivered. "Mom, I know I shouldn't interfere with wildlife, but this is an albino sea turtle. They are so rare I had to save it."

Mom's stern expression softened as she kneeled beside her daughter, examining the turtle. "An albino sea turtle...," she murmured, her eyes wide with awe. She looked back at Zel, pride mingling with her concern. "You did a brave thing, but you must be careful."

Zel nodded, her eyes still sparkling as her anxiety took over. "I know, Mom... I called the marine center, and they said drones were being sent over and not to worry... But then the turtle sank and no matter how long I waited, it didn't surface! I didn't know how long the drones would take. I had to save it! There's still some net on its neck. I can't remove it and don't want to cause more harm. Now we wait for the drones to take the turtle."

Mom sighed, handing a towel to Zel. Zel looked at the fabric, placed it on the sand, then put the turtle on it, and wrapped the towel over its front limbs.

"Thanks. Now it won't hurt itself," Zel said, hugging her close, soaking a patch of her mom's clothes.

"You've got a big heart, just like your grandma. Let's get this little one to the marine center,"

They walked back up the beach, turtle in tow, and Zel glanced at the calm, moonlit waves. A sense of peace filled her from knowing she had made a difference... And even better. The lights of the marine center drones approached.

Much later that night, after a warm shower, Zel laid

on her inflatable bed, multiple blankets piled atop her. Her smartwatch's glow illuminated her anxious face. It was 11:59 p.m. In a minute, she would fill out the most important form of her life: the Maritime Expedition Exam application. The expedition promised a coveted internship at Madlen University. Zel had tried three times before and failed. It was her last chance. A chance she shouldn't even be having. But she did.

Her fingers fidgeted, and her leg shook uncontrollably. She reloaded the page. "Sign Up Open, click here." Zel clicked. Her heart raced as the form appeared. Name, address, school—all filled out in seconds. She pasted her pre-written essay explaining why she deserved the chance, along with a brief self-introduction. As an immigrant, Zel answered the extra questions about her visa, length of stay, why they should choose her over local students, and her proficiency in Phoebian, the Venusian language.

She clicked "continue." A pop-up appeared: She clicked "I understand" and sent the application. The page reloaded, confirming the school had received her application. In four days, she would know if the school shortlisted her.

Relief washed over Zel. She couldn't believe it. She had one more chance. Zel was sure she would join the expedition. She turned off her screen and closed her eyes.

In her dream she was a demon, a red-furred dog of an unknown breed. Demon roars mingled with her thoughts, creating a disconcerting symphony. Smoke and ash filled the air, her throat burning. Everything felt real. She walked as a demon on a flower-decorated balcony under a yellow lamp.

The demon was livid, its eyes and Heart Stone glowed bright green. It watched other demons with bat wings flying overhead, longing to join them.

"Hey, where are my bow and arrow? I know you hid it!" she called. A demon inside answered, to her dismay.

"I will obviously shoot at those smug jerk's wings! That's no reason to hide it! If you were an envy demon, you'd understand!"

As the other demon answered, music flooded the place, cutting the conversation short. The world faded away like drawings on the sand near the sea.

Zel woke with a jolt, flinging her blankets aside. She hit her head on the shelf above her bed. "Ow... Shouldn't my horns be sturdier?" She rubbed her head, then realized, "Of course not. I'm human." The rock song still played from her smartwatch. She turned off her alarm.

Zel deflated her mattress, making the cramped room feel slightly bigger. The tiny kitchen had just enough space for a stovetop, fridge, and oven-microwave combo. Despite their financial constraints, her mom insisted on getting a larger place. Clothes racks filled the room, a necessity after her mom moved in.

Zel preferred routine and disliked change. She was uncertain about university and how to afford it. Zel dreaded the end of school and the start of adulthood... even if she still had three years before the end of school. She liked to plan. Failing the Maritime Expedition again would crush her dreams of studying marine biology.

The shadows of her mom and a beast with bat wings and horns moved into the room. Her mom lay on the double bed, accompanied by a green schnauzer with a reptilian tail and horns—her familiar, Luma.

"Morning, Mom," Zel said.

"Hi," her mom replied, briefly glancing up from her game.

"Morning, Luma," Zel greeted.

"Hello," Luma responded.

Sharing a cramped student flat with her mom was challenging, though she appreciated her mom's month-long journey from Earth to Venus. The distance made calls impractical, with messages taking up to thirty minutes to send. Zel often avoided her mom's bold, entitled behavior in public, feeling embarrassed... like the one time her mom cleaned her hotel room herself every day with the door wide open so the robot staff would see it and do their job right.

Many teachers discouraged Zel's dreams of marine biology and they pushed her toward more practical fields. But her mom believed in her dreams, suggesting she finish high school abroad where opportunities were better. Phoebe was affordable and offered hope.

Zel's finances were tight. The monthly allowance her mom sent her (quite a bit to cover her food, studies, and accommodation) wasn't worth much in the Phoebian currency. In fact, the last Zel checked, one Phoebian Ria was equal to almost four monetary units of Zel's country. Her finances were so tight that, once her mom learned that Phoebian culture encouraged teens starting at sixteen to get part-time jobs along with school to teach discipline and "prepare them for adult life," she begged Zel to get one to help cover the expenses.

Zel picked out a sports bra and a yellow t-shirt, then put on a jacket to cover her scar that extended from her elbow to her wrist. She felt guilty for finding her mom embarrassing, but living together was nerve-wracking. After all, Zel had snuck her mom into her student accommodation, knowing it was risky.

Despite her fears, Zel's love for the sea kept her motivated. Growing up by the ocean, swimming came naturally, even though she respected its dangers. The sea made her worries disappear. She dreamed of getting a job that let her float in the ocean all day.

Zel sat beside her mom. "Hey Zel, you should have attuned with a familiar by now," her mom said. "Luma and

I attuned on my sixteenth birthday. You've been sixteen for months. Have you had prophetic dreams of your demon companion yet? We should go to a familiar rescue center if you aren't going to summon one."

"Attuning" was a fancy way of saying "giving your soul to a demon." That was what familiars were. Demons straight from Hell. But upon crossing, they took forms akin to dogs to seem friendly. Dogs with horns, forked tongues, paws that worked like hands, pointy tails, and wild fur colors.

Zel's stomach lurched. "Yes, uh... We can go in a week or two..."

"Or we could go now," her mom insisted.

"In theory, it would be better if I had a familiar for the Maritime Expedition. But I'm not sure if now is the right time. In practice, if I show up to the expedition with a familiar, everyone will know I am too old, spread rumors about how I got in either by bribery or maybe because you took someone who works in the selection process to—"

"Nonsense. Zel, you will fit in better. You told me everyone in your class had attuned, and that you feel bad,"

"Vih hasn't," Zel said.

But Vih isn't as nervous as I am. She couldn't care less... But that's because she is oblivious... I don't want to be like that. Even though I appreciate her ability to not care.

"Zel, I can't believe you signed up again. We talked about this."

"I wasn't about to waste the chance first place in the biology Olympiad gave me! Students who participate can apply for an internship at Madlen University. I really want to study there," Zel said. "It's one of the best universities, not just on Venus, but on Earth and Mars, too."

"Zel, there are other opportunities in life. Get up, the two of you," her mom said, pausing the game.

Zel felt hurt. "Mom... I want to try this one more time."

"Zel, let it go. Things don't always work out. We talked about this. The longer you go without attuning, the easier it is for an Abomination to eat your soul. I wouldn't be able to live with myself if that happened to you."

Zel wanted to argue, but it was unwise. *I will count to five and obey my mom,* she thought. Then counted.

"Let's go, then," she said, getting up.

"Now?" Luma asked, her eyes glowing light blue. "Maybe fifteen more minutes?"

"We'll go, get my daughter a familiar, and be back in no time," her mom declared.

"But it's the weekend. Can't we do this another day?" Luma groaned. Zel agreed in silence, relieved she hadn't yet gained a familiar. It meant delaying responsibilities she didn't feel ready for.

"Nonsense. Luma, don't fall asleep," her mom said.

They left the studio, stepping into the flamboyant carpet whose wild patterns decreased the use of cleaner bots by management, and Zel locked the smart door. As they entered the corridor, the building shook with a crack of thunder. Zel fell to the floor. Her mom grabbed a wall to avoid falling. The lights went out, then flickered back on. Zel's heart pounded. Had a wrath demon had a powered flare-up? An earthquake?

Mom and Luma stood there, wide-eyed. The lights went out again, the walls trembling like a ship in a storm. Then the corridor lit up once more.

CHAPTER 2

Zel and her mom had stopped near apartment 72, its door marked with scorch and claw marks, when the lights flashed. Vines snaked out from the apartment, then the door exploded outward, sending a girl and her belongings flying. Zel squinted and recognized Vih, her classmate, covered in dark goo, her waist-long hair singed.

"Vih? Are you alright? What happened?" Zel asked, approaching. Her mom held Luma up.

"Summoning ritual went Wrong with a capital W. But I'm fine, don't worry," Vih said.

Zel hadn't spoken to Vih in months, not since Vih had cheated on that test. Vih had moved on and gained everything, while Zel had stayed behind, not angry anymore—just kind of sad and embarrassed about how petty she'd been.

Zel's curiosity grew when she noticed an e-reader displaying disturbing images of experimental summoning rituals.

"Don't get close," Vih warned. A huge vine, thick as a tree and with sharp red thorns, emerged from the door and wrapped around Vih's ribcage, lifting and waving her around like a toothpick.

"Don't worry," Vih said as the plant dragged her face along the wall. She snatched something from her belt and plunged it into the vine, making it angrier. It turned her upside down and shook her like a saltshaker, spilling her wallet, smartwatch, protein bars, and other treats onto the carpet. Once everything stopped dropping, the vine resumed swinging Vih around.

Zel stared as the vine dragged her classmate across the walls, ceiling, and floor. Luma covered her eyes with both paws. Mom ducked, hugging Luma tightly, eyes closed.

"Ah, Zel, I saw your grades on the school's wall. Congrats. You did very well in math. Among the top ten, right?"

Grades were the last thing on Zel's mind as the vine flung Vih out of the skylight, and she disappeared from view and leaving a trail of papers as she fell. The vine retracted into the apartment, closing the door. There was a click, and the smart lock turned red.

"I AM OK," Vih's voice echoed through the corridor. Zel hurried to the windowsill and peered over. Vih had landed on one of the building's safety nets far below, looking like an insignificant insect stuck in a spider's web among other miscellaneous items.

"Wow. Thank the powers for the safety nets around the buildings," Zel said in awe, her mom and Luma nodding in agreement. Even though Vih had taken her last chance, and Zel hadn't—and probably wouldn't ever—forgive Vih for that, she was glad Vih was safe.

"Should we go?" Luma asked after a moment. The three of them moved away from the window and continued to the parking lot.

Once they reached their garage, the door ascended, allowing sunlight to stream in, illuminating the AeroCar adorned with a vibrant graffiti turtle that shimmered in the light.

To Zel, AeroCars resembled a fusion of ancient drones and cars, relics she had only seen in museums. She often marveled at the bravery of those who had piloted such hazardous machines, unaware of the catastrophic impact their fuel had on Earth's delicate carbon cycle, which triggered the sixth mass extinction. The consequences had been devastating: polar caps melted, seas rose, water stagnated, sea life suffocated, and cities drowned. Up to seventy percent of life went extinct, and the desperation had driven people to make deals with demons, being who had historically seen humans as prey. Yet, that desperate time had spurred an incredible innovation resulting in the AeroCar.

In history class, Zel learned that if her ancestors had been more concerned about the climate, and corporations more willing to change, humanity might still be stuck on Earth. Instead, they had turned to space, mining asteroids and importing water from Europa. A space elevator, a monumental structure built on the equator in the Atlantic Ocean, became a priority, linking Earth to space without the need for rocket fuel.

Initially, humans controlled the mining robots via controllers, but they soon became autonomous, self-replicating, and self-repairing. Humanity developed sustainable energy sources, created machines to pull carbon dioxide from the atmosphere and turn it into calcite, and had planes pump gases into the atmosphere to cool the planet. Genetic engineering aimed to restore ecosystems by reviving extinct species. Some believed Earth was beyond saving and looked to other, like Venus and Mars.

Terraforming Venus and Mars had taken nearly four hundred years, but billions have since called those planets home.

The AeroCar in the garage had a car-like frame with a segmented, dragonfly-like tail and a propeller at the end. Four insect wing-like structures adorned its roof, painted to resemble a turtle's shell. Zel marveled at biomimicry, reflecting on how ancient humans underestimated nature's powered flight.

As the doors swung open, Zel secured herself with a triangle seatbelt while Luma nestled into a basket designed for familiars. Her mom tapped commands on her smartwatch, and the engine roared to life, casting a bluish glow inside.

"Welcome. I'm your Assistant for Driving and

AeroCar Navigation, ADAN. Where can I take you today?" a calm, robotic voice greeted them. Zel sighed, forgetting how long ADAN's introduction took after an update, one which he had received the night before.

"We're heading to a familiar rescue center," her mom said.

"Connecting to the closest location. Loading up GPS. Starting voyage," ADAN announced.

With a hum, the propeller spun to life, the wings flapped, and the vehicle's wheels folded underneath, emitting a soft blue glow. It lifted off the ground and burst out of the garage door, seamlessly merging into the flow of flying traffic.

The AeroCar glided alongside towering skyscrapers adorned with lush rooftop gardens and expansive green spaces. Dense forests sprawled below, interspersed with sparkling lakes teeming with colorful bird-life—a vibrant, natural reserve thriving among the urban sprawl. As they soared past, Zel marveled at the vast vertical greenhouses stretching upward, their crystal-clear glass facades. Within, automated fruit-picking robots moved with precision, their agile appendages harvesting oranges and depositing them into waiting baskets.

Rising above the skyline, Zel's gaze moved to the shimmering bio-dome above—a wonder of engineering and ecological preservation. Constructed from interlocking triangles, it stood as a proof to humanity's ingenuity in terraforming Venus. Yet, despite the planet's transformation into a habitable paradise full of life, the bio-domes served as a safeguard against the volatile oxygen levels beyond the city limits.

As the AeroCar cruised alongside a colossal wall, Zel marveled at the intricate mural of three demons adorning its surface. Towering figures loomed against a robin's egg-colored backdrop, a demon, an angel, and an abomination, their majestic forms evoking a sense of ancient grandeur.

Each of the three figures possessed a mesmerizing blend of features—hooves and wings—in a majestic display. One figure, bathed in an ethereal glow, bore feathered wings reminiscent of chamomile tea, as a halo floated above its head—an angel. Another boasted scales the color of raw steak, its furled bat wings cascading down its graceful form as intimidating horns and tusks graced its head—A demon.

Zel's gaze lingered on the last figure—the most imposing of them all. With four wings spreading out like the sturdy frame of a beetle's, it exuded an air of elegance. Long, twisting horns adorned its head, while gemstone-hued scale plates shimmered in the light. Intriguingly, a pair of antennas sprouted from its brow, adding to its enigmatic build. Those were the dreamer demons, but they weren't demons at all. They were abominations that filled the same ecological niche as demons, and so looked similar. Besides, calling them "dreamers" helped people not mistake them with the other abomination species that ate dreamers, demons, angels, and whole human souls.

"Hey Luma, when you're in Hell, you look like the middle creature, don't you?" Zel asked, pointing at the red figure sporting tusks and horns.

The schnauzer glanced at the mural. "I do, but my scales aren't red," she said.

Mom gave her familiar a few pets in the shoulder blades and, given the little creature's wagging tail and dreamy eyes, she seemed to have enjoyed that.

"Hey, is it true that the angels don't attune to us, ever?" Zel asked, glancing back at the creature with bird wings. Zel had heard they seldom even talked to people. They were very reserved, and never turned into dogs, unlike the other two demon varieties. Zel's teachers had said that, during the demonic exodus, angels had rejected the deal offered to the demons and suggested their own.

"Not that I know of. They are good at turning into ravens and flying about the city, collecting their share of soul power from the leftover scraps of attuning. They should all have turned into vultures because that's what they act like," Luma huffed.

Zel knew angels and demons, like Luma, had a centuries-old conflict, and it only stopped when they and the dreamer demons crossed into the human world, begging for mercy. The Demonic Exodus was a taboo, so it was better to not talk of it. Ever.

A hologram displaying "Rescue Center" and a picture of a person embracing a mutt with horns and a reptilian tail caught her eye. Zel's AeroCar flew through the projection toward the parking lot, causing the image to glitch before restoring itself.

Soon, the AeroCar descended, landing in front of a cozy, two-story building with bright blue walls and a sign reading "Familiar Rescue Center." Several families bustled about, each accompanied by familiars, their varied features reflecting their demonic origins.

"I wonder what my familiar will look like," Zel said as they left the Aerocar.

CHAPTER 3

Socks, a pride demon and English toy spaniel, sat at a cluttered vanity, grooming his long ear fur. Bottles of creams, shampoos, and bizarre hairbrushes littered the table, with photorealistic artwork depicting demons and cityscapes tacked to the wall behind it. Several colored pencils laid scattered about, too.

Socks's flattened face gave him a perpetually grumpy look, which suited him fine. He had considered venturing outside that afternoon. He craved the sun's warmth and the scent of the outdoors.

But I don't want to be seen like this, Socks thought, his reflection a constant reminder of his anger. Revenge clouded his mind. He wanted to confront the demon who wronged him, the one whose face he knew but name he didn't. That demon would pay. Dearly.

A shadow, one of a human-like figure with a halo and feathered wings, crept up the wall. Socks tensed, fearing discovery and punishment for fleeing Hell. He had gotten out using the creative interpretation of a rule. Was that the issue?

Socks turned to face the shadow and relaxed upon seeing Harper, a raven with a blue halo and a satchel, perched on the windowsill. Sunlight made his feathers sparkle, and he sported a translator collar, like Socks did. But the most interesting thing of all—his feathers were white.

"Harper," Socks growled. "I'm not returning to Hell, nor telling you where those magazines are."

"Socks? Is that you?" Harper sneered. "You're lacking your usual arrogance. Is it because of that haircut?"

"Mind your business," Socks spat, his eyes and Heart Stone glowing purple.

"You can't stay here in the human world. You rank too

high. Go back to Hell. The scent of soul essence must drive you crazy," Harper said.

Socks's eyes glowed brighter. "I am a lesser demon. My rank isn't that high. I left to escape orders and feel valued. I want to be myself. I won't steal essence... Besides... who would care if I took a little?"

"The law cares," Harper said, jumping and fluffing his feathers. "It's like taking someone's blood."

"I'm not interested in souls," Socks insisted. "Pretend I'm not here. I've been here almost two years already and have done no harm. Stop chasing me."

"You want to be valued. Do you feel valued here? Don't you know why you turn into dogs?"

"Because of an insane demon who broke a contract. The higher-ranking demons turned him into a dog as punishment," Socks explained.

"Exactly! People are humiliating you by making you into a dog. I am surprised you are fine with it!" Harper said.

In truth, Socks wasn't. No pride demon was, but since they could do nothing about it, they ignored it and refrained from discussing it as much as possible.

"Pretend I am not here," Socks repeated.

Harper shook his head, dismayed by Socks's indifference, and his eyes and halo shone bright blue.

"Can't you curb your diligence for once?"

"Being diligent is my nature, just as prideful is yours," Harper retorted. "Have you ever curbed your pride?"

Socks crossed his arms. "How do you always find me?" Socks demanded.

Harper showed a jagged, glinting amethyst-colored fragment from his satchel—a piece of Socks's Heart Stone.

Shock rippled through Socks and he stared at the shard, a painful reminder of his missing magic.

"How did you get that?" He ran his dewclaw over the

delicate broken Heart Stone in his chest, prodding the thinly protected magic slipping out of the break. It was unpleasant to do so. He rushed to the window, but he knew better than to open it.

"When you first crossed the portal. It takes a chip at everyone's Heart Stone. We keep them safe in case we need to track you down."

Socks's mind raced. "You're lying! That's like keeping a piece of someone's soul!"

"I'm the only one who knows you're here," Harper said, ignoring the accusation and pacing to the window. "If someone finds out, they'll hunt you down. If you attune with a human, your magic will be easier to track."

"That's why I'm never attuning. And I'm staying," Socks said, ignoring the pouting raven.

"So that's your plan? Living in a rescue center forever and never telling me where the magazines are?"

"Why do you want them back so badly? They're mine," Socks said.

"I misplaced a recipe among them. It was one of a kind, written by Laodamiahamadryas himself," Harper said. "It's written in ink, probably on one of the pages, or on an extra paper sheet,"

So that is what all those odd scribbles are... Socks thought. But he wouldn't let Harper know that. That magazine was his. It was a fair trade. He wasn't giving it back. But he eyed the drawer the magazines were in.

"Look it up on the internet. I haven't seen anything like that," Socks said. "Plus, I destroyed all the magazines you ever gave me!"

Save for the ones in that drawer... he thought, glancing at it again.

"I don't believe you," Harper said. "Why would you destroy them? Are you trying to annoy me?"

21

"My recent goal is to give a certain someone a sound beating, but it doesn't concern you. Now leave," Socks said.

The raven huffed and flew off.

Socks walked around his pentagonal room and picked up a pencil and paper. The moment the lead touched the paper, a knock startled him, causing his pencil to skitter across the page. He glared at the window but saw no raven. Socks knew he should wait a little longer... But he really wanted to know. He rushed to the drawer. He looked left, then right, then opened it, revealing three magazines with skylines on the cover and singed edges that stank of sulfur.

"Let's see what this recipe is all about..." he muttered, but before he touched the magazine, another knock startled him and he slammed the drawer shut. He looked at the window. Harper was gone.

"Hey Socks, it's Roxie and Brass," called a familiar voice. Roxie, to be exact.

"I'll stay in my dorm forever," Socks called back.

"Do you want revenge or not?" Brass asked. "Today is perfect for revenge."

"We won't let anyone laugh at you," Roxie added.

Socks rolled his eyes. "Right. I'll go. Do you have a cloak I can borrow?"

A package slid through the dog door. Socks opened it and grinned at the cloak inside.

—

Luma, Zel, and her mom entered the rescue center. The building's design, with its interlocking pentagons (not regular ones, duh) reminded Luma of Hell. Zel found it clever and unique. Inside, drones hovered around, welcoming visitors with blue lights on their screens. Shelves lined with demon care supplies held remedies for various afflictions.

The scene was proof of the center's popularity, with people and their familiars browsing the shelves for supplies.

Zel observed a boy in a school uniform—odd for a weekend—making a purchase for his covet demon, while others, dressed in pajamas or construction gear, mingled among the aisles.

There were so many familiars all around them. Dogs of all breeds and sizes. Zel felt nervous, not being able to tell one demon from another.

"I can't tell them apart," she confessed.

Luma gave her a smile and explained, "Corrupt demons have horns, dreamers have antlers. Heart Stone colors help too: blue for sloth, pink for covet, yellow for greed, red for wrath, green for envy, purple for pride, and orange for gluttony."

Luma pointed to lounging dogs with blue Heart Stones, "Sloth demons, like me" She then turned to two fiery-eyed dogs with red Heart Stones, "Wrath demons." Next, dogs with goggles headbutting each other with green Heart Stones, "Envy demons." Lastly, were regal dogs with feathers and venomous barbs. They bore haughty looks, and Zel wondered if they were talking ill about the other kinds.

Zel's heart raced. She knew what those were. Her hand brushed over the scar on her elbow.

"Pride demons," she muttered. "They all have venom, acid, or something worse. Let's just go around. I'm not looking to find out firsthand."

Her mom and Luma exchanged concerned glances, but neither said a thing as they veered away from the pride demons.

The center's low furniture catered to familiars, emphasizing their comfort. At the main desk, a drone greeted Zel. It looked like a ball with two bee-like wings, a screen with two lights that resembled eyes, and a tripod on the bottom half in case it wanted to land.

"Welcome. The plaza is that way," it said in a robotic voice, as it produced the hologram of a hand pointing to the enormous glass doors at the back.

"I'll wait here... try to attune with someone who already has the silver brand to avoid having to separate from them," Zel's mom said. Luma stayed too.

Zel headed toward the glass doors, which opened to a sunlit plaza. The flower beds were a paint explosion, with sunflowers as tall as Zel and flowers as big as a dinner plate, along with potted colors, posies, and a myriad of others she didn't recognize. Some walls had graffiti, others were plain. Despite the disorder—multi-colored tiles on the roofs, mismatched chairs on tables, and an explosion of plant life—the scene exuded a sense of peace. As she strolled, Zel couldn't help but draw parallels between the eclectic decor and her student accommodation, where the residents' diverse backgrounds resulted in a mishmash of styles.

Meanwhile, Socks, Roxie, and Brass moved across rooftops, Socks's hood and cape flailing. They even jumped over Zel herself.

They hid behind a roof ridge, Socks's cloak snagging on a tile. Below, the robots milled about, humans walked and the noisy birds perched on nearby rooftops. Socks noticed the envy demon sitting on a shaded bench. She was a Chinese crested dog, but the coated version. Her fur was long, silky, and bright red.

"Is that her?" Socks asked, eyes narrowed.

"Yes, we're sure," Roxie confirmed. Brass fidgeted with his spectacles. Socks doubted it. "Her horns should be bent. I remember."

"Envy demons' horns are straight. You might have been too... distracted... with... uh... all," Roxie started.

"How do you know about that? You were both knocked out and woke up tied up in a cleaning closet. That doesn't seem like you were there to see it," Socks growled, his Heart Stone flashing purple. He would make that envy demon pay for hurting his companions. Both his friends looked offended.

"We're trying to help. Don't be mad," Roxie said.

Socks closed his eyes, then tried to crush the overwhelming feeling of embarrassment and defeat. He told himself to focus on the present. He tried locking his emotions away before they made his magic short circuit, but it was like getting a beaver to build a dam to hold a flood. The little dam of sticks, twigs, and mud held the rapid erratic flood that time, but it wouldn't always be the case.

"Alright. The culprit locked you up because she knew you could stop her before she could carry out her plan. I am S... S..." Socks shook himself. He tried to say it, he did. But his magic didn't let him. It seized his vocal cords whenever he tried to utter the word. That happened with a lot of words. It took very special occasions for him to say them. Also, he didn't enjoy saying them. It forced him to admit he was wrong, which he preferred not to, even if he was. "You know what I mean," he said at last.

"We do," Roxie said, wagging her tail.

"Brass, will the plan work?" Socks asked.

"It would short-circuit my magic, so it should work on her too," Brass answered.

"But she has wings. You don't," Socks noted.

"Only difference is we brag more," Brass said, removing his goggles. "I hate these."

"Won't light hurt your eyes?" Socks asked.

"Only if I see something I really want, or if someone shines a light into my face. But I guess that hurts anyone with dark vision, like pride demons and covet demons," Brass said.

"What's the plan?" Roxie asked.

Socks's eyes locked on the envy demon relaxing with papers. "Get revenge," he said, narrowing his eyes.

CHAPTER 4

Zel walked through the crowded plaza, observing a group of children marveling at a Westie demon breathing light blue hell flames. The scene reminded her of school trips where demons would share their culture. Lost in thought, a watermelon-colored envy demon with elegant features and silky fur jolted her back to the present.

Zel approached him, unsure of how to start a conversation. Before she could muster the courage, a guy approached the demon and said something Zel couldn't hear. The familiar nodded. The guy scooted a chair over, sat down, and the two started chatting, making it seem effortless. Frustration filled Zel. For the next familiar she saw, a "Hi" would have to do.

Zel resumed walking. Other people approached familiars and talked to them normally, while she was about to break down from her shyness and nervousness. Zel struggled to push past her shyness in a world that expected confidence. She knew that while children could afford to be shy, adults would label her as aloof or rude for avoiding social interactions. Instead of understanding her hesitation, they would see her as someone who never joined workplace outings, making her feel even more isolated in a place where fitting in felt impossible.

Zel's eyes landed on a coated Chinese crested dog on a bench. Her fur was the color of roses, and she messed around with the papers. Mirrored goggles covered her eyes. She was probably an envy demon.

Zel looked at the familiar for a few seconds. "Just say hi," Zel whispered to herself before taking a deep breath and strolling toward the dog.

The dog raised her head and stared at Zel. Her tail wagged twice. Zel froze. For a moment, it was like her brain had fizzed out and she didn't know what to do. That wasn't any demon. It was the one from earlier, the one she dreamed about.

"Hi," Zel finally said

Hello, Zel heard in her mind.

"I am Zel," she continued.

The human from my dreams. I am Climenaeuploea. Call me Willow in your language. Nice to meet you in person, Zel heard. the familiar's tail wagged, for good that time.

Can you hear my thoughts? Zel thought.

Somewhat.

Willow's magic flowed through all Zel's cells, like the boost from drinking energy drinks or coffee, just stronger.

As Willow and Zel talked, Socks and his friends prepared their plan on the roof above. Roxie noticed Zel talking to their target.

"Wait, halt, stop," Roxie interjected, setting down the small wooden barrel she held. "There's a human. If we act, we'll involve her, too."

The cloaked demon bristled at the notion. If his mark attuned, she would flee before he could exact his revenge. Yet, the idea of harming an innocent bystander unsettled him.

"What?" Socks leaned over the ridge, curious.

"Perhaps you could use your pride demon natural weapon? If, say, acid dripped from the roof, she might flee," Roxie proposed.

"I can't spew boiling acid," Socks retorted, resentful.

"Then what can you do? After all this time, I can't remember you ever mentioning your power," Roxie asked, a hint of suspicion in her tone.

"We'll discuss it later," Socks deflected, realizing he should have disclosed his abilities to his friends long ago, but somehow never did.

To be fair, he had never told anyone. The ones who

knew figured it out themselves, knew what to look for, and it became obvious. Socks leaned forward for a better view.

The curly-haired girl waved her arms animatedly and Socks edged closer to the edge, hoping to devise a plan that wouldn't endanger her. Then, a part of Socks's cape snagged on a jutting roof tile and it gave way with a snap. The force holding him back vanished, sending him tumbling off the roof, his cloak unraveling as he rolled over the smooth tiles. His friends watched in concern as Socks plummeted.

Would you like to attune? Willow asked.

Zel's heart fluttered as Willow's voice echoed in her mind, her smile stretching from ear to ear. She had spent years dreaming of this moment—finding the familiar meant to be hers. Yet, since it was happening, she couldn't shake the feeling it was all moving too fast.

Will Willow get too angry if I say no? Can she hear what I am thinking right now? Zel pondered, stealing a glance at the little dog, who showed no sign of hearing her thoughts. Her mom would insist Zel attune sooner rather than later, regardless of whether it was the right fit.

"I would," Zel said. But something didn't sit quite right. Having a familiar meant a reliable companion, someone who wouldn't flake out like her friends often did. But it also meant responsibility—a constant connection she wasn't sure she was ready for.

Zel's friends had dismissed her interests in animated movies and video games, though, urging her to focus on more "adult" concerns like dating. Feeling misunderstood, Zel found refuge in her hobbies and working out as many hours as her muscles could handle per day.

Even with all her reservations, Zel knew she couldn't avoid it forever. Everyone got their familiar at sixteen. It was just what happened. And delaying it wouldn't change reality.

Willow touched Zel's arm with a paw. Zel shivered as

a chill washed over her. She felt like snow had buried her. Her soul, a shining, glowing orb, left her ribcage. It wriggled and levitated. It looked like a tadpole pulsating with magic.

Willow reached for the soul.

"Wait!" Zel called before the dog could touch it. Willow looked at her.

"I can come visit you every week... Or a few times every week... But could we delay actual attuning? There is this thing I really want to do," Zel said, and regretted it the moment she saw the expression on Willow's face.

"It is not that I don't want to attune! I just don't want to do so now be—"

A high-pitched bark got their attention. Zel and Willow startled. A dog was falling from the roof. Zel didn't get a good look at him, have time to react, or even process what was happening before he crashed on top of her and Willow.

Zel opened her eyes, finding herself on the ground with Willow's snout inches from her face, and grass tickled her cheeks.

"Are you alright?" Zel asked Willow.

"I'm fine. Are you?"

"I can hear your thoughts. You said you were hurt," Zel said, confused.

"I thought no such thing,"

The two stared at each other, confused.

"Your Heart Stone is still on your chest," Zel said at the same time Willow said, "That isn't my Heart Stone color."

"What?" they said in unison, staring at each other.

Zel's attention snapped to a high-pitched yelp echoing through the plaza. She spotted what she initially mistook for a Cavalier King Charles Spaniel, standing with a front paw raised in discomfort. Concerned, she glanced back at Willow before rising to her feet and approaching the unfamiliar dog.

"What's up with these voices in my head..." Socks

thought out loud as he shook himself and pawed his nose. *I may have hit the ground way harder than I thought... Oooow... I miss my wings... Ow...*

When the dog turned to face her, Zel recoiled in surprise—they weren't the elegant Cavalier King Charles spaniel she had expected. Instead, they were a canine with a flattened face, reminiscent of flat-faced cats. His severe underbite and eye-level nose only added to his unconventional appearances. His fur was orange like a peach, with hints of purple on his ears, muzzle, and tail, as well as a few pink markings.

"I think we attuned by accident," Zel said, showing her fractured Heart Stone necklace.

"Preposterous!" Socks growled, before noticing she had his Heart Stone.

My chance to stay here... My future... My free will... All gone, Socks thought. His dreams of living in the human world shattered. His lost friends, endless nights pouting over his lost ability to fly, and all the sacrifices he had made to stay among humans, vanished in a simple mishap. He could almost feel the searing heat of the volcano where they'd imprisoned him, burning him for eternity. The girl was still talking, but her words faded into the background. All he could focus on was the rising dread clawing at his chest.

Doubt gnawed at Zel. *What if I end up alone?* The Pride Demon would ruin everything. He'd say something crude or offensive to her friends, chase them off like every pride demon always did. He'd mock her teachers, make every small misunderstanding a battle. And he never knew when to stop, never admitted when he was wrong—just like her mom. *What if this demon pushes everyone away?* She thought of the Marine Expedition, the one dream that still felt within reach, slipping through her fingers like water.

A gathering crowd interrupted Zel's worries.

"What happened?" someone whispered.

"Is that... Socks? Can't be, right?" a sighthound said.

Zel felt overwhelmed, but it wasn't her feelings. It was the demon's, flooding into her as he grew more anxious about the crowd. The purple glow from his eyes, how he acted—it all felt wrong.

"Shouldn't you... have feathers, like those guys?" Zel whispered, glancing at three familiars in the crowd. They had long silky fur, sharp zigzag horns, and flamboyant feathers like birds of paradise. Two had a barb with a glistening black stinger on their tail tip. They moved with an air of owning the planet, so confident they didn't need to say anything. Zel looked back at the flat-faced pooch.

The zigzag horns checked out, but she saw no venomous parts, no aura of disdain. The King Charles spaniel tried to hide his face under his paws. Zel, hating the spotlight herself, felt a pang of empathy. She knew how he felt all too well and wanted to make him more comfortable. They needed to get away from the prying eyes.

Zel picked him up, placing a hand on his ribcage, the other on his hind legs, and ran. Walking might have attracted less attention, but she reached the door to the lobby quickly. She closed it behind her, leaned against it, and breathed, enjoying the calm as she crouched with a sigh.

"You can put me down," Socks said.

Zel obliged, setting him on the ground. His movements were still tentative as he favored one paw.

"So, uh... What's your name?" Zel asked.

"Socks. Latalaeumaeus if you prefer my demon language name," he said after a moment of silence. With that, he retreated to a corner of the room, pressing his horns against the wall in quiet foreboding. As she observed him, her eyes trailed down to his paws, noticing the distinct coloration that resembled a pair of socks extending up to his hocks/wrists.

She wondered if Socks had chosen his name based on them. And yes, he had.

"I am Zel. What are you doing?" she asked.

"Enjoying my free will before the razorbacks track me down and stuff me in a volcano," Socks said.

Zel had no answer to that. "That is specific. What are razorbacks?" she asked. Part of her feared he would say, "they are wild boars," then laugh at her face. She reminded herself to not be so judgy, and at least try to give him a chance.

"They are squads of great and greater demons. Their leader is always a bloodhound. They track runaway demons by sniffing out their magic once they attune. They capture anyone who isn't following the rules," Socks explained. He imagined three of them getting the call, each picking up a spiked dog collar from a hanger in the wall, then making their way to the human dimension.

"That sounds like Hell's version of immigration enforcement," Zel joked.

Socks didn't laugh, and Zel's cheeks flushed at her ill-timed joke. If it was a human-modded forum—the ones controlled by AI were more lenient—they would have permabanned her. She needed to watch her jokes. She felt sad for Socks. He may not be the familiar she expected—or wanted—to attune with, but his situation was dire. She didn't want to be with him, either. In part, because he was a pride demon. They scared her. Second, he wasn't the one in her prophetic dreams. Third, everyone in the Maritime Expedition would judge, misunderstand, isolate, and bully her because she was a little older, and having a familiar was proof of that.

They sat in silence for a while. Zel looked at her smartwatch, opened a question and answers social media site, and chose a forum about familiars.

Zel sat there and typed, "Help! I attuned with a pride

demon but I don't get along with them. I haven't studied how to treat him properly and I can't get over my fear of them. How do I prevent him from using his awful natural weapons on others, or me ever?" Then she stared at the "Post" button. A lot.

Her heart raced. It had been over a year since a helpful forum for immigrants from the same country as her had banned her, and the sting still lingered. She was really lonely and needed help. The forum for familiar care was useful too. She didn't want to be kicked from it. So she never posted. Just read—that was true for all her favorite ones.

She used to spend hours there, sharing her problems, helping newcomers to the country adjust, and feeling connected and understood. Then, one day a group of bullies twisted her words, and they banned her for violating community guidelines. She closed the tab. She wouldn't post. The forum was too useful to risk never being able to access it again. She sighed.

"Do you know if it is possible to unattune?" Socks asked.

"Do you want to unattune?" Zel echoed.

"If it is possible, yes. I don't want to risk being captured. The punishment would be awful. And I can see in your mind that you aren't fond of me," Socks said.

Guilt bit at Zel. Buying herself more time before attuning was one thing, but untuning for selfish reasons was another. Yet, if Socks wanted to unattune, it wasn't entirely selfish...Was it?

"Well... I will see what the drone has to say," Zel said, heading toward the illuminated area at the end of the corridor.

CHAPTER 5

Zel approached the reception desk, only to see her mom leaning on it, chatting to a drone. There wasn't a queue, but Zel feared her mom wouldn't care much if there were. Okay, there were other drones too. Zel stood in the doorway, wondering what she should do. Maybe she should pretend everything was fine and search it on the internet later.

"Hello, back so soon?" the receptionist drone asked before Zel decided. She looked at Socks, who looked grumpy and unwilling to help, still sitting in the corner.

"I have a hypothetical question," Zel said, rubbing an arm as she approached. "What if someone... hmm... attuned by mistake?" Zel asked.

"You unattune," the drone said.

"That simple?" she asked.

"Yes,"

"No strange rituals?"

"Yes. But it would get problematic if we unattuned you two here in the lobby. Come to the veterinary side of the facility with me and I can help you cut the thread between your soul and his magic," the drone said as it hovered closer. Zel blinked, then grasped the gem. The moment she touched it, she heard whispers. Likely, Socks's thoughts. They faded when she let go.

"We shall do no such thing," Socks said, leaping out of the shadows into view.

"You attuned to that familiar?" the drone asked in its flat voice, flying closer. "Where did you find him? Nobody has seen him for weeks."

"Nobody's seen you for weeks?" Zel echoed in disbelief.

"That doesn't matter. When we unattune by cutting the thread, it puts a strain on our Heart Stone. Mine is

35

compromised. If it breaks, I am doomed, since my magic will scatter all over the place. Now let's find a bunker to live in forever," Socks said, grabbing Zel's pant leg, right above her sock, trying to drag her. Given Socks's lap dog size, he wasn't successful. She stood where she was, puzzled.

"Move!" Socks demanded.

"I know a bit of magic. You said they can only track you because your magic is showing. Let's say we unattuned... and somehow did that without damaging your Heart Stone further. Would your magic disappear from wherever it is now?" Zel asked.

Socks's eyes lit. "It would. Then, I'd only need to lose the razorbacks. Which is a near-impossible task."

"But you unattuned before, didn't you? Or else you wouldn't be here, in a rescue center," Zel said. Socks narrowed his eyes. They glowed bright purple. The color of royalty. She felt bad for asking. Zel could tell it was something he wasn't keen on mentioning.

"Look at the Heart Stone," Socks said.

Zel followed the instructions and lifted the pendant with her hand.

"See those jagged edges?" Socks said.

They looked irregular and sharp and glowed.

"It's not stable for attuning. Been like that since I crossed," Socks said.

Oh... He never attuned... Zel wasn't too sure what to make of that, apart from the fact that she sometimes wondered why they didn't include Finagle's law (which, ironically, was always mistaken with Murphy's law) in physics.

Luma pondered, tapping her tail on the floor. Her eyes lit up like the sun, and she grinned. Socks hoped she had figured out how to solve all the problems in the universe.

"I know a solution," Luma said.

Socks and Zel both looked at the schnauzer.

36

"A Sealing ritual,"

"A what...?" Socks asked, frowning. He had seen one before, but it was for the dead, not breathing, walking demons in good health. Maybe Luma meant another ritual with the same name, because the sealing ritual he was thinking about wouldn't help.

"A Sealing Ritual is a ritual where someone replaces a familiar's Heart Stone. I saw it on a vet sitcom once. The one problem is that not everyone can do them. And finding a Heart Stone replacement is no simple task. They spent most of the episode building up tension and stating how complicated it was, but hey, they made it work in the end."

"Yeah. Medical dramas are a good, reliable source," Socks said, sarcasm dripping in his voice.

"I am sure a handful of research goes behind similar media. They may have embellished it, leveled to 'TV show drama,' but they didn't completely make it up," Luma said, tail wagging as she smiled and tilted her head.

Socks opened his mouth to argue.

"Please let me talk," the drone said, flying higher.

Since no one objected, it continued. "That plan would never pass legal. Everyone would say you two should stay together and learn to get along. But, if you want to check with someone who performed the ritual, an intern here claims to have. Their name is Koa. They used to work at Town Square's Trashmart's cafeteria. Morning shift. Go check if they're still there."

Zel's stomach tightened. Trusting new people, letting them in on her ideas—it felt like a gamble. Those she thought who had her back had betrayed her before. What if it happened again? Still, maybe facing a small scrutiny could spare her from something far worse on the Maritime Expedition—where the stakes, and the judgments, would be much higher.

"Hey, Mom, can you please give us a lift to the Town

Square?" Zel asked.

"Before you go, since you attuned with a familiar, I need you to fill out a few forms," the drone said.

Zel sighed, then noticed something glowing in her familiar's neck from the corner of her eye. "Whoa, what's that glowing in your throat?" Zel exclaimed in alarm, rushing toward Socks. "Have you swallowed something you shouldn't have?"

"Don't be so concerned. It's your soul. Which is in my soul pouch," Socks clarified, demonstrating by inflating a balloon-like object between his neck and chest, showing Zel's soul within. Familiars, akin to kangaroos, sea otters and platypuses, have pouches. Except, a familiar's pouch is on their throat, close to their Heart Stone, and it carries living souls, not younglings. The pouch looked way more like a magnificent frigate bird's than a kangaroo's.

"Now, can we get on with our mission? We're on a tight deadline here, and failing to meet it won't end well for either of us. It will be even worse if this deprives me of my revenge," Socks said.

"You must fill out the forms and update your documents before leaving," the drone reminded her.

Zel took a deep breath and turned back, following the attendant, with Socks rolling his eyes and growling in annoyance before joining them.

CHAPTER 6

Harper lifted his gaze from his recipe book to watch Zel and her grumpy familiar walk past the window he had perched in, following their every move. He fluffed his feathers until he looked like a white pinecone, eyes narrowing with disdain. He put the book back in his satchel. The book. The most important book of all time. It held part of Dryas's—Harper's nickname for Laodamiahamadryas—knowledge to gather souls like the great demons of the past. But it was incomplete. Since Dryas' death, Harper had worked to uncover the secret formula, the recipe. If he succeeded, they would hail him as a savior, basking in the glory of having saved angel kind from starvation, a plight since attuning began.

Harper clicked his beak in frustration, letting out a loud, harsh call. Spreading his pearly wings, he took off noisily, heading toward the nearest skyscrapers. With effortless grace, Harper soared through the air, his wings slicing through currents with the precision of a seasoned aviator. Below, the city sprawled, neon signs casting vibrant hues against the glass-plated buildings.

Despite the mesmerizing view, Harper couldn't shake his gnawing annoyance. He reached into his bag and retrieved something resembling headphones, which he secured on his head. Extracting a squarish box—an enchanted counterpart to a smartwatch—he prepared to contact Hell, a dimension accessible only via demonic magic.

"Hello?" answered an orange demon in Hell, his true form on display—hooves, wings, tusks, and thick scale plates. Surrounding him, demons milled in a lava-lined shopping center.

"Hi Rubicallophyris, we need a change of plans," Harper stated, making a sharp turn to avoid a building.

"Hi Harper. Since I'm taking Castan's place and shapeshifting into him, call me Philenorbattus, or Castan, if you prefer his human-world name. His colleagues might notice I'm a shapeshifter if you keep using my real name," Castan said, a hint of amusement in his tone as he stopped at a display window to observe hoof boots.

Harper stifled a sigh, irritation mounting as he continued his flight. "How are things going so far?"

"Not too bad. I've gathered some valuable intel," Castan said, his voice drowned out by the cacophony of a crowded food court.

Harper winced when a burst of noise assaulted his senses, throwing off his flight path. "Where are you? What's with all the noise?"

"In a shopping mall. Spark insisted on trying the new ice cream parlor for lunch," Castan explained, scanning the crowd for his companions.

Harper clenched his beak. "I find it poor manners to call other demons by such mundane names given by humans."

Castan chuckled, "They've chosen their names, like you did, Harper," he said, making the raven seethe.

"What's the problem?" Castan asked.

"Socks attuned to someone, and I still haven't located all the stuff I gave him. We need to know where those magazines are if we plan to incriminate him. Also, I think I misplaced Dryas's recipe among those human trinkets," Harper said, observing the AeroCars and humans below.

"Dryas didn't write the recipe. He lied. We should have ensured he wrote it before getting rid of him. I can look like Dryas, sound like him, and even rule Abundance like him, but I can't manipulate soul essence like he did," Castan said.

"And now Hell is going to starve if we don't find out how he extracted essence from souls. Abundance's population grows by the day, with desperate and malnourished angels from everywhere knocking on our gates. If there's a chance Socks might have the recipe stashed somewhere, we need to try. I've filled my diary with failed attempts... Dryas's knowledge about souls must have originated from somewhere. It's only a matter of time until we find it."

"Anyway, you said Castan works in a razorback team, right? Get that team on the case and get to Socks before anyone else. Sabotage Castan's team if you must. At least, don't let anyone stuff Socks in a volcano before we can set him up to take the fall for our plan," Harper said, glancing at a few lampposts, contemplating landing but deciding to keep flying to release built-up tension.

"Socks and Castan were friends. Shared a place. The superiors would consider him too close to the case and never let me on it," Castan said.

"The friendship can give you leverage in talking to Socks. Assign Castan's team to the case, make it so not all group members have to be in the same room to receive the order, shapeshift into the demon who will pass the order," Harper said.

"Someone will get punished terribly for passing an order like that," Castan noted.

"Just make sure you aren't the someone when they decide to punish them."

"Alright. But Harper, my team is that team. Keep that in mind," Castan said.

It took a couple of wing beats for Harper to understand. His eyes bulged. "Wait, that team? The one who designed a makeshift catapult to launch ammunition into an enemy stronghold, but it malfunctioned, flinging them in random directions and into various inconvenient but somehow safe locations?"

"Yes, that team."

"The same team that set a trapdoor under their target,

but activated it early, sending them plummeting into an over-the-top pile of pillows?"

"Yes. They are also the ones who set up an intricate magical trap to capture a rogue demon that backfired, causing a series of small explosions that left them covered in soot and singed fur. They have a thing for over complicated elaborate traps, because Chili is a Trap Master," Castan explained.

"I see that. Do so anyway. I don't think we have a choice. If you want to be optimistic, their incompetence might help our cause," Harper said.

CHAPTER 7

Zel stood before the colossal tablet, her fingers trembling as she entered the final details. With a heavy heart, she tapped the button labeled "Next," bracing herself for the inevitable. The screen blinked, and a resounding check mark appeared. Confetti showered the screen. "All done," it declared. To Zel, it felt like her future was "all done."

"Great! We will wrap and deliver your familiar's belongings by drone this afternoon," the drone informed before departing.

"We have to unattune before the Marine Expedition... assuming I get approved," Zel said.

"Let's go, before the razorbacks find us," Socks said, tapping a paw.

Zel hesitated, her gaze fixed on the screen as if willing it to change. "Just a moment," she murmured. There was one more thing she needed to do before they left. It felt crucial.

Socks bristled beside her. "There's no time for this," he said.

"I know you are worried, but that envy demon deserves an explanation. I'll be quick," Zel said, walking faster.

"It isn't important. Let's unattune," Socks insisted.

Zel reached the door. She held it open for Socks, but he sat by it, shooting her a look that might melt glass. "You can come with me if you want," Zel said, but he shook his head.

He seemed quite insecure about being looked at earlier... Is that why he doesn't want to enter the plaza? Because he has no feathers when all pride demons do? If so, standing there in the lobby might not feel great for him either.

"Go talk to my mom; she'll let you wait in the AeroCar," Zel said before walking away.

Willow plodded across the pinkish cobblestones, head

low. Hearing footsteps, she stopped and looked behind her when Zel approached.

"Zel?" Willow's voice was soft and sad.

Zel kneeled beside Willow, their eyes meeting.

"It's not what it seems, Willow. I'm not leaving you," Zel said. "I'll fix this, I promise. Then I'll come back for you."

Willow's tail wagged. "You seemed happy to go with him," she said, hurt in her tone.

Zel flinched. "I panicked. I should have said something. It was a mistake."

They embraced, and Zel felt belonging mixed with farewell. She held Willow as long as she could. Eventually, she had to let go. With one last look, Zel turned away, pained to leave Willow behind.

The red AeroCar with turtle prints stopped at the drop-off point in front of Trashmart. Zel and Socks jumped out, walking toward the automatic doors under the Trashmart sign.

Zel and Socks entered, the bell chiming. Shelves lined the aisles, drones zipping overhead. Socks looked grumpy, but Zel tried to start a conversation.

"Did you know Trashmart once got sued over their slogan?"

"No, and I don't care. I'm not keen on needing help, so save your fun facts," Socks grumbled.

Zel took a deep breath. She knew Socks was on edge. She should have given him space. The silence grew awkward.

Zel didn't like asking for help either, but for different reasons. While Socks was too prideful to accept help without a tantrum, Zel feared getting tricked or scammed. As an immigrant, people often tried to cheat her, assuming she didn't know the laws. They'd underpay her, sell her faulty goods, and exploit her inexperience.

Walking into Trashmart to meet Koa, Zel felt like a

lizardfish approaching a reef full of cleaner wrasse. Lizardfish sought the little fish to eat the parasites off their scales, like an AeroCar wash without the technology. But there was a catch. The bluestriped fangblenny, an orange fish with blue stripes, mimics the cleaner wrasse. When a lizardfish approaches one for help, the fangblenny bites off a chunk of its skin instead.

Zel didn't know if she'd encounter the human equivalent of a cleaner wrasse or a fangblenny. That uncertainty made her anxiety skyrocket every time she needed help.

They walked toward the crowded food court, hovering long armed robots picking up dirty dishes. The place smelled of ground coffee and toast. Zel approached a self-order kiosk.

"Hello?" she said. A hovering robot approached her, carrying plastic trays.

"Hi. What can I help you with?" it asked.

"I want to see Koa."

"Koa's shift ends in two hours."

"But it's important. We need to talk now," Socks said.

Just as Zel was about to suggest they wait, a bold voice cut in.

"Ignore that scrap pile. I'm over here,"

They turned to see a person with light brown skin and rainbow-colored hair, wearing a brain interface link—a common device for those who worked in AI that allowed them to access the robots—that looked like half a headband and a Trashmart uniform. They were fixing a robot, tools in hand.

At their feet, a border terrier with fur like a child's drawing of a night sky—dark, bright blue, with huge orangish stars, one of which was atop of his left eye—followed them, their tail wagging. A fan of soft, long feathers sprouted from his tail base and weirdly, from his shoulders too. He had a deep transparent scar on his chest that allowed Zel to see his beating heart pumping magic all over his body. His horns were straight, and his eyes were a yellowish green. Zel had never seen a familiar like him before. It was a little odd, even. She had no clue what his kind might be. She even wondered if he was an angel instead. One that was falling. All demons started as angels, but their angelic nature got twisted and corrupted so much overtime they literally grew horns, had their feathers fall off, broke their halos, and got evicted from their home.

"I'm Koa. They/them. What can I help you with?" the figure said, getting up. Zel wondered if she should introduce herself with pronouns, too.

"Charmed to meet you. Name's Star," the blue dog said after the long silence that followed Zel's hesitation. His accent struck her as odd—not like any demon she had heard. Maybe it wasn't the accent, but the flowery way he spoke, his words honeyed, and his voice wrapped in silk.

Socks's eye twitched; he didn't like that smooth tone. Zel wasn't a fan, either. Most familiar magic made people feel a deep-rooted fear, but Star lacked that imposing aura. Instead, Zel felt like she could trust him, as if they had been friends for years.

Stop wondering if they are a fangblenny and say something! she thought.

"Nice to meet you. I'm Zel, and this is Socks."

Koa glanced down at the dog. His lack of typical pride demon features, like feathers and venom, made him a curiosity.

"What's his natural weapon?" Koa asked.

"Come closer to find out," Socks dared, beckoning Koa with a claw, who wisely stayed put.

They turned to Zel instead. "You were looking for me?" Koa asked.

"I heard you performed a Sealing Ritual once."

Koa paused. "If you came here to ask me to do one, sorry, but it's not happening."

"You see, Socks wasn't meant to become my familiar," Zel explained.

"And you plan to have someone resurrect him after you commit murder?" Koa spat.

"Not that sealing ritual," Socks said.

"Socks said his Heart Stone is about to break. He wanted a Sealing Ritual for when we unattune," Zel said.

"That is impractical, risky, and insane. There must be a miscommunication. Suck it up and get along with him. Wait a year or two. If you still don't get along, wait a few more years," Koa said.

"If it serves as consolation, see Star? We are not a good fit. We can't unattune. Here's why. This is Star's Heart Stone," Koa said, showing their necklace to Zel. The border terrier looked insulted. The stone was a green flat gem with flickering zig-zag markings suggesting his magic wasn't stable.

"What's his kind? I can't tell," Zel asked, eyeing Star.

"A gluttony demon," Koa said. Zel doubted that. A lot.

"That green Heart Stone tells me otherwise. He should be an envy demon. Keyword 'should,' because he isn't," Socks said.

"Now that we've talked, leave," Koa said.

"But I need your help," Zel pleaded. "You must be an outstanding student to pull off a Sealing Ritual like that."

"That flattery won't change my mind. It's a risky, ridiculous idea, and I want no part of it."

"But Koa, if she knows someone who can unattune familiars with unstable magic, maybe we could get help too. I loathe it here. I miss the heat, the bubbling lava, and most of all, my friends and the food. You also want to—" Star said before being interrupted.

"Woah. It's a bit early to hurl all my motivations at them. They're strangers," Koa spat.

Zel felt for the odd-looking demon. She had never experienced strong homesickness, but she had classmates and work colleagues who had. She only missed the food and her family, things she had learned to deal with.

Socks blinked. He had heard that many demons became homesick after moving to the human plane. They missed everything that made Hell, well, Hell. Some got so sad they got depressed or returned. Sometimes, Socks missed it too. He missed the hot wind under his wings, the sparring matches, even the terrible heat, but not enough to head back.

Koa closed their eyes and fidgeted with the headpiece of their neural interface. "Where do we even get a new Heart Stone? It's risky and terrible for us too, Star."

"I don't plan on getting anyone killed," Zel declared, hands on her hips.

Silence filled the room, broken only by Star's laughter. Soon, he rolled on the floor, overcome by amusement. Koa wore an amused expression, too.

"I'm serious..." Zel said, puzzled by their reaction.

"Then you'd have to disrupt the ritual in multiple ways; it's like trying to defy physics," Koa explained. "So, listen here, Fel—"

"Zel," Zel interjected.

Koa didn't bother correcting themselves. "Unless you know someone capable of breaking magic, it's impossible."

Breaking magic, huh? she thought. "I'll introduce you to a friend of mine," she announced with a forced smirk. She disliked smirking, but it proved a point. In truth, she feared said friend never wanted to see her again... And she didn't want to see her either.

"Good luck convincing Socks to let me tag along. Demons of his kind seldom accept help," Koa said.

"I'll reason with him," Zel said, looking at her companion. She would talk to him as soon as she figured out exactly what to say to navigate his pride and convince him that accepting help wasn't always bad, even if the helper was rude... And sometimes a bluestriped fangblenny.

CHAPTER 8

In a secluded, office-like cave in Silverworks, Hell, an envy demon named Chili, a covet demon named Spark, and Castan sat on chairs. Before them stood a high-ranking greed demon, projecting a graph. It showed a plateau of high numbers with very few drops, until the middle where it plummeted straight down, plateauing at zero.

The greater demon pointed at the drop with a stick. "What happened here? You guys were a great team! Why have you been failing so much?"

"That's when Chili started leading," Castan said. His colleagues shot him sharp looks.

"What?" the greed demon seethed, stepping closer to Castan. "You are the leader. You lead and you mustn't transfer your responsibility. But if you do, perhaps it's time to consider worse punishments than vammuling to ensure you stay in line. And maybe I should punish your subordinates, too. They know better than to perform a job that's not theirs." She blew sparks of golden hellfire from her nostrils.

Castan didn't seem impressed, but Chili's eye twitched. "He's kidding!" Chili said. "He should know not to joke in front of his superiors." She glared at him. "We just had a few technical issues..."

The greed demon wasn't convinced. "Whatever is going on, fix it. If anything goes wrong on the next mission, I will punish you three. Understand?"

They nodded.

"One more thing. Chili, I have noted that you've been acting a tad bold for your job lately, as if you were in charge. I want to remind you that you aren't. Any more boldness, and we will deal with you."

"I understand," Chili said, swishing her tail.

"I won't let us get punished. We will prove our worth. I won't lead you wrong!" Chili told the others as they walked through the busy corridors of the Silverworks, past towering stalactites, other employees, and constructs. Screams from the torture chambers echoed through the hall, and Chili feared she'd join them. She just wanted to be a good leader, but she had no idea of what she did wrong.

"You always say that, and you somehow lead us even worse. So much so that I bet if we did the exact opposite of what you say, we'd succeed," Castan said, earning pointed looks from his colleagues. "Now I must go. I'll see you when you receive the mission and we need to cross to the human realm," Castan said, pushing into the crowd before taking flight.

"Wait! All of us need to be together for the briefing!" Spark called. Castan was gone.

"Don't worry. There isn't one; he's being mean," Chili said.

Chili had to swallow those words ten minutes later when they got called for a mission briefing. Without Castan. They met him again before crossing to the human realm, though.

In a graffiti-covered alley, a flickering orange light revealed the silhouettes of three horned beasts with wings. They emerged from behind a dirty dumpster and transformed into a bloodhound, golden retriever, and a muscular Tosa Inu. The trio wore spiked collars and had blank, soulless eyes.

The leader, Chili, the bloodhound, sniffed the ground and wrinkled her nose. "Can't say I missed this place. But hey, good to be back," she muttered.

A white raven with a dog collar perched on a lamppost, scribbling in a diary. Noticing the group, it closed the book and looked down. "I wasn't expecting to see THAT team," Harper remarked from atop the light.

"Hm. I see poisonous rumors about my team have

reached this world too. Don't believe that nonsense. I am Chili, and I'm here to clear that reputation!" declared the bloodhound. Her fur was acorn on top and yellow underneath, with piercing green eyes.

"This is Spark. She knows the art of portals," she continued, gesturing to a red golden retriever with tiger-like stripes. "And this is Castan," she said, pointing to the muscular Tosa Inu with green fur and a yellow-orange underbelly. A trail of silky feathers cascaded down his back in various shades of blue.

"I gather you're Harper. We heard you have a Heart Stone piece of the familiar we need to track," Chili stated.

Harper unfurled his wings and landed. "They informed me that Castan is the leader. Why isn't he the bloodhound?"

Chili's eyes narrowed. "I lead just as well as he does," she retorted, stomping her paw.

Not if the graph has a say on it... she thought. But she couldn't show weakness in front of whoever they were.

"I didn't say you didn't. I said Castan is the leader, according to the documents," Harper clarified.

Castan stepped forward. "Cas—I let her lead when we're out. It's good training," he said.

Harper raised an eyebrow. "Really? Does it have anything to do with being afraid of her?" Harper asked.

Chili growled. "You think I lead by coercion?"

"Not quite. He avoids confrontation. Last time he fought a demon like you, it got ugly. For him. So, he lets your kind do whatever you want," Harper said.

"Not true!" Chili growled, though doubt crept in. She looked at Castan. "It isn't, right?"

"Of course not," Castan replied, though he winked at Harper, confirming Harper's theory.

"He'd be too prideful to admit it," Spark added.

"Not helping!" Chili growled, but knew it was true.

"I want you to succeed. So I will offer a word of advice," Harper said. "I heard you are a piece of work. Your biggest problem is that you aren't a team player. Learn to ask for help. You are an envy demon. Asking for help shouldn't be as hard as if you were a pride demon. Listen to your colleagues... and obey your actual leader."

Chili narrowed her eyes. She listened to them! Sometimes. Okay, not too much. Maybe she could afford to listen more. Or not. Leading was all about control, not about arguing over who had the best plans or complaining. You couldn't control those who offer advice, because that implied friendship.

"A leader who always needs help to get out of trouble is weak, and a leader who isn't feared isn't respected," Chili said.

"Listen to Castan if he decides to do his job. Should I fetch a pair of goggles? Maybe one for Spark, too?" Harper asked.

Spark flinched. Chili loomed over Harper, who flew back to the light post.

"I have no need for those, neither does Spark. And Castan has as much dark vision as her. Why not offer him those ridiculous things, too?" Chili spat, huffing. She twitched her nose and sniffed the air.

Harper wouldn't answer that nonsense.

"We're tracking a pride demon. What are his natural weapons?" Chili asked after the silence grew.

"I... don't know his power," Harper said, handing her the purple Heart Stone piece.

Chili examined it. "Half a Heart Stone. Is he alright? How did this happen?"

Harper had hit Socks with a tranquilizer dart as soon as he crossed the portal. While Socks was out, Harper flew down, holding a chisel and a magical device. Initially, he intended to take Socks' magic print for tracking. He had considered sending Socks back to Hell, but that would strain their fake friendship, and Socks had valuable information about the magazines. Angered by Socks's reckless behavior, Harper had hit his Heart Stone with the chisel, intending a small punishment. Instead, he split the Heart Stone in half.

"No idea," he lied.

Chili sniffed the ground and wagged her tail. "Got his scent," she said and her eyes flashed green.

CHAPTER 9

Zel stood on the worn welcome mat in front of unit 72's battered door, her heart racing. She felt guilty for not reaching out to Vih sooner. She was about to ask for a favor after weeks of silence. Zel debated how to start—an apology, a casual greeting, or an excuse.

Socks, beside her, licked his chops a lot, as if something bothered him.

"Bad taste in your mouth?" Koa teased.

Socks glared.

"Accept it. We'll be spending a long time together. Who knew you'd need my help?" Koa said.

Socks grimaced.

Zel had assumed the phrase "the bitter taste of humiliation" was a figure of speech, but, looking at Socks, it seemed a genuine statement for pride demons.

Zel shot Koa a reproachful look. "Stop tormenting him," she said, protectively.

"Dear, wash the bitterness off," Star offered, offering Socks some cartoon bone shaped candy from who knows where. Socks turned away, refusing.

Zel sighed and gathered her courage. She rang the doorbell, her palms sweaty. She couldn't believe she was about to face Vih after everything.

When the door opened, Vih greeted her with a warm smile.

"Vih, hey," Zel said, spreading her arms. "I came to check on you due to... earlier. This is Socks, Koa, and Star. Mind if we come in?"

"Come in," Vih said, holding the door open. They walked past potted plants and shelves filled with jars, terrariums, and ceramic bird statues.

"I see you attuned to an angel. Must be rare," Vih said to Zel. Star flinched, and Socks cocked his head.

"That purple Heart Stone stands for humility, right?" Vih asked.

Zel's eye twitched, and she felt a pang of nervousness. She remembered when she had offended a host by accident.

Zel sat at the table with the family hosting her, a plastic chair wedged in for her. They all ate something called "marinated glass caribou," even though it had neither glass nor caribou in it. Zel was still sure she mistranslated the name. She felt out of place. It was her first time in a new country, and her grasp of the language wasn't very good yet.

"This is really good. Who cooked it?" she asked, wanting to give a compliment.

The room went silent. The eldest kid gave a small, uneasy laugh.

"I did," the mother said, her tone sharp, eyes narrowing.

Zel's stomach dropped. Had she offended them? She scrambled to fix it. "It's delicious."

The tension broke as the family laughed, and Zel forced a smile to join in. She still didn't know what she'd done wrong. Maybe her tone had been rude?

She hoped Socks wouldn't react like the host mom had.

To her relief, Socks laughed. "Me? I'm a pride demon. We look different without feathers, don't we?"

"Your kind has amazing powers. What's yours? I don't see any of the obvious tells. Which is weird, given that most tells are impossible not to notice. I suppose you could have fangs. That would be hard to tell because I would need to see you with an open mouth..." Vih rambled.

Socks narrowed his eyes and exchanged a glance with Zel.

"I like to keep that a mystery," Socks said. Zel could feel his resentment.

"Keeping secrets, huh? But seriously, you've got to tell me—I'm curious. I mean, people say I'm nosy, that I need to mind my business, but it's not about that. If someone doesn't want to tell me, fine. I just really like knowing how things work, you know? Nonfiction is kind of my obsession. But, okay, I do talk a lot. I get that. People don't always say it to my face, but they zone out, and that's when I realize I should probably stop. Only... I always have something interesting to say, so it's hard to just—well, shut up," Vih continued, her curiosity overflowing. Zel's heart raced, fearing Socks might lose patience and use his natural weapon on her.

"Hey Vih, how about we talk? It's been so long," Zel interrupted, forcing a smile.

"Good idea. Have a seat," Vih said, gesturing to the couches. "I'll get us tea. Zel, care to help me?"

In the communal kitchen, they stood by the 3D food printers. Zel's palms sweated.

Vih retrieved an antique tea set, using her smartwatch to unlock her cupboard, her movements graceful. "I never thought you'd attune with a pride demon. Tell me how you two met," Vih said, preparing the tea.

"Neither did I," Zel confessed. She knew she owed Vih an apology, but hoped Vih would apologize first.

"Why am I making small talk? You're here because you want something," Vih said, and her observation added to Zel's discomfort.

Zel hesitated, unsure of how to proceed. "No... I..."

"You've been ignoring me, then you show up with a stranger. You need something from me," Vih continued.

Zel recoiled from the sting of Vih's accusation. "I wasn't... I'm not... I was... guilty..." she trailed off.

Zel counted to five to recenter. As she counted, memories of their shared dream to attend university resurfaced, rekindling the betrayal and resentment that burned like a hot coal.

Zel and Vih had poured their hearts into studying for the Maritime Expedition entrance exam, but they faced failure time and time again. The previous year, Zel sacrificed everything, dedicating every moment to preparing for the exam. But disaster struck on the eve of the exam when Zel lost her school tablet with all her notes. Panic set in. Vih helped search, but they couldn't find it.

When the exam results came out, they devastated Zel when she learned she had failed again. Vih, however, had passed. While sitting in Vih's room, Zel's world crumbled. In a half-open drawer on Vih's bedside table, she saw her lost tablet with her unmistakable sea anemone cover. The realization hit her hard. Anger surged through Zel. Her friend had stolen her notes and cheated. Zel punched Vih, threw her laptop to the floor, and stormed out.

Zel still thought Vih had cheated, and the main reason she didn't talk to her afterward was the guilt she felt about hurting her friend and breaking her laptop. She regretted her impulsive actions, wishing she could go back and make a more assertive choice.

"We often see each other in the corridor. Do you know how many times you said hi to me? Once. And it was today. I always said hi to you," Vih said.

"Vih, I'm sorry. I overreacted and I shouldn't have hit you. I ignored you because I didn't know how to apologize for something so obviously wrong," Zel muttered.

The tea machine whirred, filling the teapot with a golden-green liquid that Vih then placed on a tray. "I'll help, but I'm still mad at you. Mostly, I want to have a better look at Koa's familiar. He's so odd-looking. Helping you is an excuse to tag along," Vih said, though Zel sensed Vih genuinely wanted to reconcile.

"Hey, Vih, could you add extra sugar to Socks's teacup

without him seeing it? He might appreciate masking more of the bitterness," Zel said.

Vih sighed and poured the tea. "It's tricky to be kind to pride demons. They see kindness as charity. You must make it look like an accident," she said and added the maximum amount of sweetness the pot allowed. She placed the teapot on the tray with six teacups and returned to the living room.

Koa sat on an armchair, Star in a familiar basket attached to it. Socks examined a bookshelf, careful not to touch anything. Vih set the tray on the table, and Koa put their smartwatch away. Zel took a seat, and Socks rushed to her.

Vih poured the tea and handed a cup to each guest. Koa made a disgusted face and spat out the tea into a napkin. Star grimaced.

Socks took a sip, and comfort visibly washed over him. His tail wagged, and he stopped flicking his forked tongue as he lapped the tea.

"What is this made of? Sugarcane? Sugar beet?" Koa asked, enraged.

"I am all for confectionery, but this is just awful," Star complained.

"It seems to be a little too sweet, like soul essence," Socks said, pushing the teacup away. The group looked at Socks in shock.

"Soul essence leaves a sour aftertaste," Star said.

"Never thought I'd meet a demon from Abundance, the city ruled by Laodamiahamadryas. It's known for its sour souls for all to eat," Socks said.

"That's forbidden!" Koa exclaimed. "Demons can't feed on soul essence anymore. That was the deal for letting you take refuge here. You now feed on the magic souls radiate! It is the whole reason behind attuning! You get fed, and both humans and demons get protected from abominations."

"Can you blame us for craving a sip of its deliciously

61

rich power?" Star asked. "In the past, soul essence was our sustenance. It fueled our existence, allowing us to maintain our true forms and master ancient angelic... or demonic arts. The essence of a single soul is enough to transform us into our true selves. Now I'm craving it. Do any of you volunteer a smidge of soul essence?"

"Star! No!" Koa said with a pointed look.

"Sorry, Star, but my soul tastes awful," Vih said with empathy, though Zel disapproved. "Please don't try the arts or any other magic foolery in my living room. There are enough holes in here already."

"What now?" Zel asked, shocked, noticing the black gaping holes in the ceiling.

"The demonic arts, my dear. We wield the magic of possession, shapeshifting, portals, and more. The truce forced us to forget these traditions, leaving us weaker and yearning for our past glory," Star said, looking down.

Zel could tell he resented the loss. She had read about the arts and demons who delighted in tormenting souls had horrified her. Perhaps it was for the best that they couldn't possess people anymore.

"The past is over-glorified," Socks said. "The demon hierarchy was strict. Constant wars. But portals and shapeshifting still exist, though rarer now." He glanced at Star. "For example, rumors say Laodamiahamadryas can turn into a person."

"That's forbidden," Vih exclaimed, eyes wide with fascination.

"I must correct you, dear. He could not shapeshift at all," Star explained.

"Who was this city ruler? Did he have a short nickname?" Vih pressed.

"His friends called him Dryas, if you must," Star said.

"Dryas despised humanity," Socks added.

"Despise is too strong a word," Star countered.

"Where did all the food come from?" Vih urged.

"The ruler claimed to have a font of soul essence, but no one saw the source," Socks explained.

"It was an essence spring. He built the city on top of one," Star interjected, rubbing his eyes.

"Studies showed that wasn't the case," Socks countered.

"Was he a good leader?" Vih pressed on, oblivious to Star's discomfort.

"Um... how about we talk about something else?" Star tried to change the subject.

"Those who met Dryas said he was kind," Socks continued. "He was a kind angel, but as far as rulers in Hell go, he was above average. Liked by many, though prone to flights of fancy affecting his financial judgment."

"He was not prone to flights of fancy," Star said defensively, to Zel's surprise

It is almost as if Star is... Hmm... Zel thought.

"But he had secrets," Socks pressed. "The soul essence had a sour note, like candy coated in citric acid. And his mysterious trips and unusual death—impaled in the heart."

"Don't remind me," Star pleaded, raising his paws.

Everyone stared as a thick aura settled in the room. Zel forgot she shouldn't and took a sip of tea to distract herself, but found it nauseatingly sweet. She grimaced and set the teacup down.

"Please don't mention it," Star said, calmer. Zel feared Socks might, but the spaniel stayed silent.

"Zel, let me explain our plan," Vih said. "We'll begin with the unattuning ritual. When Socks's Heart Stone shatters, we'll enact the Sealing Ritual." She paused. "These rituals date back to when our species were adversaries, and a demon physician named Mittreiargema crafted them."

Her words hung in the air for a breath, then she

continued. "During a war, humans had a weapon: the silver bolt ballista. It could pierce a demon's Heart Stone with lethal force. Mittreiargema discovered how to preserve life by channeling the magic surge into another Heart Stone. Her studies saved many demon lives."

Socks coughed, his collar lighting up as he struggled to speak. "That Sealing Ritual? No. Zel, we are sticking together. Forever. Let's find a bunker... Great choices: dragged back to Hell or having my Heart Stone explode," Socks said.

"It might not," Vih tried to be optimistic.

"What Sealing Ritual did you think we meant?" Koa asked.

"Probably this one. I based my knowledge on a TV show," Zel confessed, understanding Koa and Star's reaction at the Trashmart. She felt silly for suggesting a Sealing Ritual for a living demon.

"Don't worry. I will control the ritual. I can bind your magic to your body to prevent it from dissipating. Koa is a vet; they know their stuff," Vih said.

"Unlike you, I am guessing," Socks said. Vih's face darkened.

Socks, don't talk to her like that. She's trying to help, Zel thought, staring at Socks with folded arms. He looked away, tail lashing.

"Vet student," Koa corrected.

"Two problems: getting the ritual right and avoiding an elite team. For the latter, we need friends in the smuggler's market. They might have Heart Stones for sale. We also need to hijack ADAN's route system. The place is rather... illegal. Good thing we have someone who is into robotics!" Vih said. The group turned to look at Koa.

"What?" they asked.

It wasn't long before they all stood in Zel's garage and watched Koa hold tools Zel wouldn't dare guess the name in their mouth, sitting on the AeroCar, trying to pry something off the panel.

"Hello. If not done correctly, disconnecting ADAN from the vehicle will damage it. There are better ways to fix errors," said ADAN, in its robotic voice. "You are using the wrong protocol for deactivation. I will check for errors. Check complete. I found no software errors. Please, if there are hardware errors, take the vehicle to an authorized repair cen—"

Koa disconnected it from the wires, and it made a weird noise as the sound faded into silence.

"Taking off the whole thing is easier than hijacking it. I'll drive. Where to?" they asked.

CHAPTER 10

They drove past the greenery-covered city and parked near a busy café. Vih led them to a hidden manhole, pried off the lid, and revealed a round slide—like those in water parks, but dry and dimly lit from above.

Just like that, the five slid down the slide. Zel fell onto a soft old mattress beneath the chute and thanked the powers above. She got up and dusted her jacket off. Koa's screams got louder, and before Zel knew it, Koa flew out of the tube and crashed into her. They barely stood again before Vih collided with them.

"Ow..." the dark-haired girl complained, before getting up. Koa groaned and stood. Vih got up with the finesse of someone who had done that a million times.

Zel found it hard to believe her eyes. It was broad daylight, but where they landed seemed like nighttime. Everything was dank. Neon lights flickered on and off, and silver ravens flew everywhere. One raven carried a bundle of thick, dark paper in its claws. Rusty catwalks loomed above them, some so high they faded from view, leaving only colored lamps visible. Ahead of them laid a very busy market.

"This way. I'll introduce you to Hawke, a friend of mine. If someone can help us, it's her," Vih said, pushing past an awe-struck Zel and an indifferent Koa and taking the lead.

Lots of booths surrounded them. So many they created cramped corridors, and the sellers tried to lure them in by claiming their products were the best in the entire market. But with every seller saying that, at least a few were bound to be lying.

Paraphernalia blocked the streets. Stalls had raised their curtains. Each had a silver raven and sold unique items. Zel spotted one with scrolls. Scrolls made of actual paper.

Another kiosk traded keychains. They looked ordinary enough, but if a silver raven sold it, that meant things weren't so simple. There were even sonic stunners and electroshock rods for sale among the magical objects.

"Look at all that magic paper for demonic deals. I always wondered what Harper did with the scrolls," Socks said, eyeing the thick, dark bundles of scrolls many of the ravens had for sale, or carried in their talons.

"You know an angel named Harper?" Star asked.

"Do you?" Socks shot the question back.

"If that Harper is Dryas's friend and a diligent angel, then yes, I do know him. They always told him not to sell things here, though. If you gave him a deal paper, does that mean all those magazines he stashed were yours?" Star asked.

"Might he be, unless he traded with someone else, too," Socks said. "How do you know about that?"

"I, uh... was very close friends with Dryas," Star said.

They didn't convince Socks.

"You traded magical paper for... magazines? That is... interesting. May I ask why?" Zel asked.

Socks eyed her, as if considering if he should answer or not. "They assigned me to work in architecture once. I got to glimpse a picture of human construction and the smooth curves on all buildings amazed me.

"So I started seeking magazines to build visual databases and draw inspiration from them. Then, your culture intrigued me, leading me to want to know more about humans... speaking those... Hey Star, you said you were close to Dryas. Do you remember if he ever wrote an important recipe in one a magazine? A magic recipe of sorts? Harper was looking for one," Socks asked.

"Oh, that old recipe... I recall something about it. But you see, Dryas had his reasons for keeping it close. He feared Harper's enthusiasm for vammuling could lead to...

unforeseen complications," Star said.

Zel, distracted by Star, bumped into someone. Her cheeks blushed, and she worried they'd scold her for it.

"Oops, sorry," she told a guy with a grumpy look before moving out of the way as fast as she could. He seemed annoyed, but soon disappeared into the crowd.

Phew... He must have been in a good mood to say nothing.

"What is vammuling?" Koa asked.

"A vammul is a very common demonic punishment, and every demon goes through it at least once. It is the punishment for being incompetent and everyone makes mistakes," Vih explained.

"Who, erm... vammuls... the highest-ranking demons?" Zel asked. If there were no ranks above them, she doubted they would be subject to punishment.

Star looked annoyed, but Socks seemed somewhat amused.

"As Vih said, it is a punishment for being a terrible boss. If a demon receives a sentence for it, it isn't the rank above who punishes him, but the one below, and not just anyone punishes, it's specifically his underlings," Socks explained.

"Okay, you demons made it even worse," Zel said, shocked. She wouldn't have the heart to hurt anyone, ever, but there were times she felt her boss was an absolute donkey, and she had a coworker or two who wouldn't hesitate telling him so if they could do so without consequences.

"And it gets even worse. The tool used for disciplining in such situations is built to cause the most pain without cutting through their thick scale plates, or causing injury. That means someone can wail down for pretty much as long as they want," Vih said.

"I think they made it better. Whoever is underneath wouldn't dare hurt their boss in fear of retaliation," Koa said.

"There are loads of safeguards to prevent that. Hey Star, are you Harper's boss?" Socks asked.

The border terrier looked insulted. "What makes you think that?" Star asked.

"Sorry, let me ask that again. Was Dryas Harper's boss?"

"Why do you ask? Curiosity getting the better of you?" Star asked.

"I was wondering how Dryas concluded Harper could get overenthusiastic with these things," Socks said.

Star looked as if he would jump on the other dogs' throat and start a fight.

"Let's get going, please," Zel said, and thankfully, the others complied.

Vih led them through the maze with a GPS. Despite the crowdedness and the overpowering smell of oil and grease from the food stalls, Zel knew the long lines were a proof to the tasty eats.

"Woah. I never thought I'd witness angels engaging in so much illegal activity," Star said, surveying the diverse range of products.

"I seldom expected to see so many feathered ones," Socks said, scrutinizing each stall owner.

Zel and the others snickered. Socks did not find it amusing.

"I am talking about their shadows. They all have halos and feathers," Socks said.

Zel directed her gaze to the tent draping. All the ravens had a humanish shadow with wings.

"Back in our homelands, most of them shave their feathers because of the heat. I heard that a very long time ago, we demons had them, too." Socks said.

Star stumbled before staggering forward. "I daresay you haven't had the chance of encountering many angels then," Star said.

"I am sure I know more of them than you do," Socks said.

Star smirked. "Doubtful. I assure you, they don't shave their feathers," Star said.

"Most of the ones I've crossed paths with were featherless. My workplace was full of 'em," Socks said, his memories vivid.

"I've heard of angels being punished by working alongside your kind. Stripping an angel of their feathers is disgraceful," Star explained.

"That explains why they're all side-eyeing me," Socks said, his gaze narrowing.

Star scanned the area, noticing the curious stares directed their way. Ravens whispered among themselves, and a group on a nearby catwalk erupted into laughter.

"I don't think they're staring at you, but me. Koa, lend me your jacket," Star asked, trembling. Koa obliged, draping the coat over Star's shoulders.

As they continued their stroll, Socks noticed a decrease in curious gazes aimed his way, affirming Star's suspicion.

Then the group walked past a curious stall.

It had no neighbors. One side featured an enormous robot claw, while the other had a pile of scrap-filled boxes. The owner, a raven with a red halo, pecked at a piece of machinery arm that ended in two prongs. The crowd avoided it and the ravens overhead made detours. Zel noticed Socks was beside her, but Star was way back, looking at them from a distance.

"What is up with you? Get over here!" Koa said.

"Can't," Star called back.

"Can't? How come Socks can and you can't?"

"Silver," Star said as shivers went down his spine. Zel recalled the metal's powerful magic and how it burnt not only a demon's skin, but their magic, leaving deep, green scars that never healed.

"Silver?" Socks asked in awe, then had a good sniff. "Yes, I sense it now. I guess I spent so long as a silversmith, I got desensitized to how uncomfortable standing next to it is."

"A silversmith? In this time and age? Why not get a construct to work for you?"

"A demon silversmith is a soldier, not an actual silversmith. They got that nickname by treating silver to grant the permanent residency visa to demons who want to stay in the human dimension," Vih explained.

"I heard about that... Instead of getting a digital document, like we do, demons get branded when they get a visa," Koa said.

"Not every visa, just the permanent one," Socks explained.

"Dears, I am still waiting back here, and I won't be getting any closer to that stall!" Star said, and the group walked back to him, and Vih led them through another route, to avoid the lonely stall.

As they passed a stall offering scrolls and magical objects, a vendor extended a wing, beckoning Zel with a gesture. She wanted to approach, maybe examine a few items... but hesitation held her back. What if she broke something? No, better not to risk it. Magic items weren't cheap.

Vih guided them to a stall that dwarfed its neighbors, its ornate lilac curtains standing out among the market's drab hues. The stall boasted a diverse array of wares, from fruits suspended in macrame hangers to illicit weapons bundled in the back. Clusters of dark, thick paper laid stacked to the side. At the center of it all perched a pudgy golden raven, adorned with a golden smartwatch on one talon and rings on each claw of the other.

Zel couldn't shake the unease gnawing at her. Unlike the other sellers who exuded trust, that raven instilled a deep-seated fear within her and lacked a halo.

Her gaze drifted from the preening bird to its shadow on the wall, a looming silhouette with bat wings and horns.

"I thought angels had feathers and a halo," Zel said, scratching her chin.

"Hawke is a greed demon," Vih explained.

"But a raven?" Koa asked. Vih shrugged.

The bird raised her head, then sprang to her foot. "Your companion is a dog. Given who he is, it is an interesting sight," Hawke said.

Star flinched and hugged the jacket closer. If Koa were drinking, they would have spat it out. They glanced at the border terrier. "Are you implying something?" Koa asked.

"Let's not jump to conclusions," Star said, attempting to diffuse the tension.

"Hello, Hawke," Vih said, approaching, trying to amend the ill start.

"Greetings. What brings my best customer back so soon?"

"Yes, see, we need a bit of a rare thing. A Heart Stone. One for a Sealing Ritual." Vih said, a shy smile on her face.

Hawke narrowed her eyes at both Socks and Star. Her facial features flattened as much as possible. "Can't sell that," the bird lamented.

"And selling these is fine?" Socks asked, motioning to the myriad of magic artifacts like scrolls, stones, and jewelry scattered all over the place. Hawke ignored that.

"The replacement stone is for me," Socks said, fluffing his fur. "It wouldn't be bad faith. Tell them you saw the silver brand," Socks said, extending his paw, exposing the etched symbol on his palm.

"Is that..." Hawke started, eyes broad.

"The marks that silver branding leaves on us? Yes," Socks said.

"Only demons allowed to stay in our world forever get

73

that brand," Zel echoed.

But if he's allowed to stay, why are the Razorbacks acting like he isn't? she thought.

"How much?" Koa asked.

"What?" Hawke asked, ruffling her wings in anger.

"You are a greed demon. How much do you want?" They folded their arms.

"I cannot be bought," Hawke declared, puffing her feathers like a peacock and strutting around. Socks snorted. Star gave her a very odd look.

"Sure thing," Koa said. Vih was the only one who showed no sign of doubt over that statement.

Zel felt like most of her classes and self-studies on demon kind were thrown out the window. Perhaps demon nature wasn't so set in stone as humans believed. Maybe they could change for the best, instead of following their instincts and being utter jerks. Socks gave her a side-eye.

Then again... Maybe not.

"But, if I accepted bribery, which I don't, you couldn't pay my price anyway... But I will see what I can do. Stand here," Hawke said, flying off with the grace of an eagle, heading for the distant catwalks above them.

She left the group staring at one another.

"Do we just wait?" Star asked.

"I guess," said Vih.

CHAPTER 11

At the other end of the market, Chili, Castan, and Spark roamed the tight passages. Chili, being a bloodhound, kept her snout low, tracing the potent scent snaking across the ground. Her tail thumped in anticipation. The aroma grew stronger the closer in proximity to their quarry they got. As they passed, ravens scattered, their cries rising above the commotion. Nearby, a stall owner startled before retreating, leaving a scattered mess of feathers.

"I've heard tales of these places. How do they smuggle all this?" Spark asked, her tail swishing. She approached a nearby raven, causing it to shrink in terror before vanishing through a portal and leaving contraband behind.

"They're fortunate we're not in the business of dismantling their operations," Chili said, her focus on the scent trail hidden among the overwhelming magic saturating the air.

"These miscreants tarnish angels' reputation. They should be ashamed of their actions," Castan seethed.

Chili marveled at how the silver ravens withstood his gaze without disintegrating. "That's unlike you," Chili noted, the tension rising.

"You're presuming to know me better than I know myself," Castan retorted.

"That sounds like you," Spark chimed in, tail wagging. "You'd say 'the angels critique our deeds, causing inconvenience, yet they indulge in the very behaviors they condemn. Their virtues are but a facade, hoping we remain oblivious to their schemes. We must expose their hypocrisy, confront them, and assert our authority,' " Spark recited, mimicking Castan's tone, her tail swaying with her steps.

Chili veered left, the scent overpowering. They were on the verge of catching their culprit. "Spark, you sound more like Castan than Castan himself," the bloodhound said, earning a laugh from Spark while Castan kept his stoic facade.

"I have a plan. We turn right here and we could—" Castan started.

"No! I have a plan and I say we go straight!" Chili said, jumping in front of Castan, hackles raised. "We are going to follow things by the book! If there is a method, it means it works and we must follow it or else we will fail!"

"Aha... Tell me, when was the last time doing things by the book worked?" he asked.

"It would have! If everyone had listened and things went according to plan and—"

"We go right, now obey me," Castan said, turning right.

"Wait! Castan!" Chili called.

He kept going. Eventually, she and Spark had no choice but to follow.

CHAPTER 12

Meanwhile, a few stalls down the bazaar, Zel tapped her foot, Socks feigned boredom, and Koa stood with arms crossed. Vih, however, couldn't resist peeking at nearby goods. After what felt like an eternity, a golden flash streaked back, clutching a tiny, ornate thing in its talons.

With graceful precision, Hawke landed, flicking the box open with her claws. Inside, there was a bright, semi-transparent rock. It was round and flat and smooth, akin to pebbles that wash on a beach after millennia of erosion. The surface glinted, and it had an ethereal glow.

"A Heart Stone," Hawke said, fluffing her feathers.

"Woah," Star said, eyes huge. Before anyone could do anything. Dozens upon dozens of ravens with silver wings flew off screaming, creating a cacophony of chaos.

"Razorbacks!"

"Greater demons!"

"Run!"

Ravens from nearby stalls scrambled to pack items in a frenzied manner. Others flew off, abandoning their booths with a heavy sigh, knowing there was no point in trying to save it. Socks trembled. Zel felt his fright flooding in, overwhelming her senses; he wanted to bolt and hide for infinity.

"Business is closed," Hawke said, giving the group in front of her a glare.

Vih reached to snatch the container.

"PAYMENT FIRST!" Hawke said. Her eye's bright golden glow danced, and she pecked at Vih's fingers.

"Ow," Vih said, retracting her limb and placing the hurt finger in her mouth.

"There is no time. We pay later. Give it to us," Vih said, tasting blood.

"I don't sell on credit, not even for you," Hawke said. "Meet me at the meeting spot. Tomorrow at noon. Bring the payment, and I will bring you the goods, DO NOT BE LATE." She shut the box with a talon, spread her mighty golden wings, and took off, looking like a small beacon. She blended into the unkindness, despite her bright coloring. Zel only heard the demon shrieks.

"WAIT, HOW MUCH ARE WE PAYING?" Zel shouted, cupping her hands around her mouth. But it didn't work. The raven was long gone.

"I will assume the usual," Vih said

A kiosk next to them exploded in pink hellfire. The heat burned something deep within Zel, not just her skin and clothes. It differed from regular fire, but couldn't tell why. She screamed and ran the opposite way, to a blue draped stall. That one blew up, too. Zel spun, aiming for the narrow passage, but boxes ablaze in fuchsia fire fell into the narrow corridor, blocking their path. She stared at them, mouth agape.

Three huge, muscular horned dogs appeared from the last side, running full tilt at them. The canines circled the group, using the fire as an ever-growing barrier to keep them trapped.

"We can and will use lethal force! Don't move!" Castan threatened.

"Your familiar's a runaway. Or, in your terms, an 'unlawful non-citizen.' We're here to extradite him from your realm. Hand him over," the bloodhound said, staring at Zel. The envy demon had been polite, but her companions growled and bared teeth.

"Put your knees behind your head and get down on your hands," the golden retriever said, wagging her tail. Her colleagues gave her a bug-eyed look, and the leader facepalmed.

Zel kneeled and put her hands on the back of her head. Koa did the same.

"Psst, guys, you are doing it wrong," Vih whispered. She had contorted herself in a yoga pose so crazy it was a miracle her pants didn't rip.

"Spark, get the prisoner," Chili ordered. The golden nodded, then darted forward.

Socks closed his eyes in resignation, bracing himself for whatever fate awaited him. But to his surprise, Spark bypassed him, seizing Star in her jaws instead.

"That's the wrong one," Chili said as the golden approached.

"But he has no silver brand," Spark said.

Chili sat and grabbed Star's wrist, examining his palm. "This is odd. He's masking his magic. I can't tell his kind," Chili said, letting go and grabbing Star's horns. "He looks like an envy demon, but off. His eyes are the wrong color. They look yellow. Ours are always green. And those feathers on his tail make no sense,"

"Maybe he has mixed magic?" Spark said.

Castan rolled his eyes as Chili stiffened a laugh, not wanting to upset her friend.

"Nope. Those don't make it to his age," Chili said.

"Looks like a kindness angel to me. One that grew horns and lost his halo, but didn't fully turn into a demon yet," Castan said.

His work colleagues glanced at each other, then looked at him. Zel was quite puzzled herself. She looked at Koa. They didn't seem surprised.

"But isn't the halo the very last thing to go?" Spark asked.

"Could I look?" Castan asked, stepping forward, trying to break the discomfort.

Star cowered in front of such an imposing dog. The Tosa grabbed him by the horns, and the blue dog did his best to hide any emotion. Castan glanced at Star's shadow and used a claw to tap Koa's Heart Stone twice.

"He is a kindness angel for sure, but his halo is missing. Which is odd. Hold him down, I want to check his heart," Castan said, walking away from the humans.

Horror washed over Star. Chili held the border terrier and the greater demon used a paw to push Star's chest fur away, as Star tried to not squirm too much in discomfort. Castan discovered a literal hole in Star's chest. It had several cracks coming from it, like lightning bolts, and was big enough it was possible to see the border's terrier heart beating through.

"Woah. I have never seen this in my life," Castan said, eyebrows shooting up.

"I remember seeing something like it—a scar. Poor demon got skewered at a weird angle. Missed her heart by a hair's breadth," Chili said.

"But it hit him dead center... How could it miss the heart?" Castan asked, then he checked the demon's back and found a similar scar.

Castan used a claw to touch the rim of the heart opening. Star's eyes watered and he writhed, snarling. Chili and Spark glared at their companion with squint-eyed looks.

"Stop, you're hurting him," Koa called.

The Tosa shot the vet student a disdainful look.

"What did you do that for?" Spark asked, offended.

"Sorry. I was curious if it was real," Castan said.

"Maybe I should poke your heart out of curiosity and see how you feel about it. What's wrong with you?" Spark growled.

"Spark, we'll sort that out later," Chili said. "Wait... Castan, did you just apologize?"

The bulky feathered dog shrugged.

Zel's mind raced with possibilities. With a desperate plan forming in her mind, she seized the opportunity. A covet demon, a pride demon, and an envy demon comprised the razorback team. They all had eyes sensitive to changes in light because of their dark vision. The bazaar was a dim-lit place. Maybe she could...

She activated her smartwatch's flashlight and cast its beam into the darkness.

The glare startled the greater demons, buying Zel and her friends precious seconds to escape. They bolted past their stunned adversaries, their hearts pounding.

"Get them," Chili yelled.

Zel squeezed through the panicked crowd, running as fast as she could, with Socks close behind.

Zel's heart raced, the razorbacks closing in. She'd hoped they'd stay incapacitated longer. Then they vanished in a puff of light, reappearing in a different passageway. Then, with another flash, they materialized right beside her, and the stall that had been there collapsed in a shower of splintered wood and pink fabric.

She stumbled back, eyes wide in terror, running the other way, only to have a geometric portal that shimmered with swirling colors like a mesmerizing lava lamp stopped her. Sharp shards shot out from the square, followed by the razorbacks cloaked in pink.

As the portal vanished, Zel surveyed the wreckage behind her, the stall reduced to a heap of broken beams. Curiously, its fabric covering was missing.

"The art of portals! Amazing! How do you do that? What does it feel to go through a portal? Can I cut something in half by running it through the edge? Oooo, what if something goes wrong? Will you get stuck inside a wall? I read a lot about this art. Some say—" Vih started, her eyes huge with wonder, until Castan walked up to her.

"Quiet," he growled.

Vih placed both hands over her mouth. Her awe at the razorbacks' portal magic baffled Zel; how could she be curious in the presence of such terrifying creatures that wished them nothing but harm?

"I can cut things through by placing them at the portal's edge," Spark whispered to Vih once Castan walked away.

"Hand over your familiars." Chili's growl shattered the tense silence, but Koa hugged Star. Vih had no familiar to worry about.

Zel hesitated. It wouldn't be fair to Socks to just hand him over.

"I think you've got the wrong familiar," Zel said.

"My nose is never wrong, human," the bloodhound scoffed, but Zel pressed on, directing her attention to Socks. He displayed his palm scar, evidence of his lawful status.

"We would be punished if we let him go. And until proven otherwise, he's guilty," Spark interjected, her tone firm.

"You two talk too much," Castan snarled, charging at Zel.

CHAPTER 13

Zel's heart raced as the hulking Tosa Inu approached, its feathers shimmering in the dim light of the bazaar. Then a rogue beam of light struck the creature's face, and it yelped and stumbled to the ground.

Startled, Zel and Socks turned to see Koa wielding their smartwatch's flashlight like a weapon, while Vih did the same to Chili and Spark, who whimpered and pawed at their faces. Heart pounding, Zel rose to her feet.

"Who knew such a silly idea would work?" she pondered aloud.

"I almost feel sorry for them. It's terrible when that happens," Socks said.

A few days prior, he had been in his room, drawing, and it had been quite dark, but he couldn't be bothered to turn on the lights since he could still see fine. (Ok, he'll admit the colors were all wrong when he checked his artwork later.) Then Roxie and Brass came over to visit. Roxie mentioned how dark it was, how she couldn't see a thing, and turned on the lights, and Sock's reaction hadn't differed from the one the razorbacks had. Not to mention that the world looked sparkly for a few minutes afterward.

I didn't know his kind was capable of compassion... Zel thought.

"Run!" Vih's urgent command spurred them into action. They dashed toward the nearest stalls, Vih aiming the flashlight behind them. Koa caught up quickly, leading them to a blue kiosk tucked between large crates. A sleek scooter leaned against the wall, and Koa crouched down, trying to get it running.

Star's green glow threatened to give away their hiding spot. Socks scoured the shelves and crates, finally pulling out a small cylinder. He tossed it to Zel.

Zel turned it over in her hands, spotting the pin and a lever labeled "Smoke Grenade."

She hesitated. Koa jumped in, keeping their flashlight pointed at the razorbacks.

"I got the scooter working. Hop on before I leave without you."

Socks shot Zel a frustrated glance. "Throw it! If you don't, they'll track us and start messing with portals."

Zel's doubts gnawed at her, but there wasn't time to second-guess. She pulled the pin and threw it, releasing a thick cloud of smoke. Zel climbed onto the scooter with Koa and Vih, grabbing Socks before they sped into the bazaar's winding alleys, the headlight slicing through the haze.

Vih's voice cut through the chaos. "We need to reach the catwalks on the other end and climb. It's the only way out." She guided Koa through a reckless turn and a pile of crates crashed through a portal ahead, shattering on impact.

Zel's senses sharpened at the deep, monotone howling, signaling the razorbacks' relentless pursuit. Castan, the Tosa Inu, caught up with their scooter, ramming it with all his weight. Koa sped up, veering toward several stacks of crates for cover.

The dog caught up. With each collision, Zel's nerves jangled. Castan took a deep breath, then aimed his fangs at them.

"Watch out," she cried.

Vih's swift kick sent Castan reeling, his attempt to unleash his powers thwarted.

Castan stumbled and Chili rushed to his aid, concern etched on her face. Zel sensed a flicker of sympathy from Socks, a genuine concern for their foe's well-being. It sparked an idea.

"Use one of your amazing natural weapons," Zel urged Socks.

His reaction puzzled her. "My natural defenses won't be very helpful," Socks said.

"How about shooting quills?" Star suggested.

"THOSE AREN'T Q—" Socks snapped, his eyes and Heart Stone glowing with irritation. Zel sensed his annoyance and said nothing, dropping the subject.

"Prepare to jump," Koa said.

"Off a moving vehicle?" Vih asked, worried about the danger, potential injuries, and lack of knowledge in performing such stunts. Koa rolled their eyes and hit the brakes, allowing the others to leap from the scooter just before it careened into the stack of crates, which toppled over one another, creating a barrier as they ran off.

Chili halted, causing the golden retriever and the Tosa to collide with each other. The bloodhound stomped a paw in rage once she realized the crates had trapped them. She howled, and the team realized their target had escaped. Without knowing which way Zel and her friends had gone, teleporting would be futile.

Vih led them along endless catwalks and winding corridors, some so dank and dim her flashlight was necessary despite Star's glowing patterns and Socks's insistence that he could guide them. When Zel got annoyed at her familiar's stubbornness on guiding them despite not knowing the way, she realized it was Sock's way of saying "Your flashlight is hurting my eyes, turn it off!" She understood his nature, but she had hoped he would be at least more straightforward when he asked for help. She turned her flashlight off. When Koa asked, she simply said that their and Vih's flashlights were enough.

After what seemed like an eternity, they reached a latch, which Vih worked at until it yielded, flooding the darkness with a cylinder of light. Star was the first to emerge into the twilight, followed by Socks, then the humans, stepping into a parking lot with Zel's AeroCar in the distance. Nearby, a table occupied by three individuals and their families gawked at them in astonishment as Zel waved before they continued on their way.

Socks admired the deep purple sunset above the buildings. He had heard that Venus had the most beautiful and intense sunsets of all because of its atmospheric composition.

Centuries prior, humans had constructed a massive mirror to block out the sun and freeze its inhospitable atmosphere. If left alone, a day on Venus would last 243 Earth days. But clever humans added another set of giant mirrors to mimic the circadian clock on Earth. Socks found the idea absurd, even more so because it worked, giving them sunsets with purple and green splashes. As he looked at the black outline of the buildings, the group walked toward the vehicle and he hurried to catch up.

"Hey, why are they called 'razorbacks'? Aren't they offended at being called pigs?" Zel asked.

"I know the answer to that!" Vih exclaimed.

"I'll be surprised when you don't," Zel said, warmth filling her before lingering feelings of guilt, and maybe a smidge of resentment toward her friend, overshadowed it.

"Demons, in their true forms, make pig noises," Vih said.

"Only to your puny human ears," Star retorted, surprising Zel with his uncharacteristic rudeness, leaving Socks and Koa shocked.

"Once, razorbacks borrowed essence to keep their true forms so they could have an advantage in searching for the fugitives. They got nicknamed razorbacks because it didn't end well for the ones who straight up called them pigs. Overtime, because of widespread use of the term, it stuck as their official name, even now that borrowing essence got outlawed," Vih explained, undeterred by Star's remark.

They hopped into the AeroCar and locked the door.

"So, I guess we will head home and meet tomorrow again," Koa said.

"Do you think the razorbacks won't find us there? Magic sticks. They'll track my magic to a home where we have been and lie and wait there till we return. It is just not safe. We need to stay on the move," Socks said.

"Vih lives close to me. Might not be such a good idea for her to go home, then. Koa, could we sleep at your place?" Zel asked.

The vet student snorted, then laughed. "Wait, you're serious. No, you can't. First, I don't want to be here, I don't want to help you, and I don't care what happens to Socks. I want to go home, work on my personal robotics project and study demon anatomy. Second, I live in a homestay."

"Isn't the host mom traveling for work this weekend?" Star asked, hopeful, before getting a "shut up" look from Koa.

"We should find a hotel," Vih said, kicking the AeroCar into drive. The cabin lit up in a blue glow.

"Yes, I'm sure every inn will be open to host three minors without their guardian's consent," Koa spat.

"Some student accommodations allow minors to stay with only a letter from their parents. Hotels may work the same," Zel said.

They took off, merging with the city's Saturday evening traffic.

A small, squarish building with a round neon sign that read "Motel" sat at a corner in the road. Zel's turtle-painted AeroCar parked in front of it.

Inside the resort's spacious lobby adorned with intricate wood carvings of jaguars, ducks, and cranes, the group passed a holodeck where patrons wearing virtual reality goggles cheered. Forklift-like robots navigated the corridors, ferrying piles of luggage.

"Seems like a nice place," Vih said, eyeing the facilities.

"I smell food. Can we eat first?" Star asked, wagging his tail at Zel.

Approaching the reception, Zel requested a room for three, only to receive a rejection because of age restrictions.

Their next attempts met similar fates, each venue denying them accommodation because of age. Exhausted, they returned to the AeroCar, their quest for lodging futile.

"I'll try calling my mom. I'm sure she is going to help," Zel said. She stepped out into the chilly night breeze and dialed her mom.

"Hello, Zel! Where are you?" her mom asked when she answered. "I was worried. It is getting late. What time will you be home?" she asked, holding the smartwatch camera closer to her face.

Luma appeared in the frame, too. "How did it go? Have you found the vet?"

"I have, yes, but it isn't quite solved yet... I'm calling to ask..." Zel's words got stuck. She had no clue what to say when her mom asked why she couldn't sleep at home. Then there was the whole 'I'm sure they won't find you here. Come home' false reassurance she'd give. Zel didn't feel like her mom would understand, or help if she told the truth.

"I want to spend the night at Vih's friend's house. Is that alright?" Zel asked. She felt terrible for lying.

Zel wanted to be truthful. It was her mom, but she feared to have her problems and fears dismissed. Zel already felt aimless in life. She didn't need to feel worse by having her familiar taken from her.

"It's good to know you two have made up. Send me the address as soon as you can, alright?" her mom asked. "Ah. One more thing! Your familiar's things arrived. He must be quite the artist! Look at all these pencil sets." Her mom showed off their foldable table packed with pencils and pencil cases of all colors and shapes. "There's also this magazine. It is one of a few, but this one has a bookmarked page." Her mom picked it up. It had a skyline on the cover, and part of it was seared. She flipped it open on a page full of scribbles clearly scribbled in ink on top of the original. "I wonder what it means. Luma said it's in Demon, but she can't read it right. She thinks it's a magic formula. Now I have to go, share your live location with me the whole time."

"Alright. Love you, Mom, I have to go, too," Zel said.

"Love you, too," her mom said. Zel hung up, sighed, then walked back to the AeroCar, opening the doors upward and slumping in the seat.

"My mom is... busy tonight." Zel said.

"What about your two's parents?" Socks asked, looking at Koa and Vih.

"My parents live in another city. Sorry," Vih said.

"Same," the vet student said with a sigh.

"Also, Koa, could I please have your address?" Zel asked.

"What for?" they spat.

"My mom asked for it... How about we stop somewhere for dinner, then go then sleep in the AeroCar? It is spacious," Zel said.

CHAPTER 14

They pulled up to a Burger&Burger, its neon sign blazing 24-7 high above like a beacon.

Inside, the warm yolk-colored walls enveloped them, silent robots bustled about, and self-checkout kiosks buzzed with activity. Families and friends filled the tables, chatting. Zel and her companions found a table in the back, but were unaware of the whereabouts of their familiars, save for the memory of Star's playful antics.

"Growing up is sad, isn't it? Hard to believe this was our last summer break," Zel said, dipping bread into a pool of melted cheese. "Now it's all work, all year. Weird, right?"

"You'll adjust. But summer will always be a sanctuary from the cold, long hours," Koa countered, bitterness lacing their words. "I sometimes regret fast-tracking through school. Lost my freedom and ended up with more work."

Zel's thoughts spiraled, and she rubbed her neck, anxiety filling her. Koa's words echoed her deepest fears—growing up, losing her parents. The mere thought paralyzed her.

"And university?" Koa pressed. "What's the plan?"

"I want to study marine biology, maybe extend my visa..." Zel said. "I'm trying to join this year's Maritime Expedition. This is my last chance. I hope I make it. I need to unattune with Socks if I do. Everyone will poke fun at me! If I have a familiar, they'll know I'm too old to be there, and they will be mean and say I bought my way in, or that I'm a fake... Connections are everything. If I'm attuned to him, I don't think I'll make any good friends or get the most out of the Marine Expedition. Part of me fears they won't even let me in if I have a familiar!" Zel confessed.

She didn't need to mention that she thought of herself

as an official failure at sixteen. But she looked at Vih to see if the latter would have a reaction, but Vih acted like Zel had said nothing. Zel had hoped she would at least be sorry or show regret.

"False hope is a cruel thing. Sometimes others fool us into having it, but when we fool ourselves, it's a problem." Koa said.

Zel could tell it was genuine curiosity, but their tone hurt her feelings a little.

"It's a legitimate second—well—fourth chance! I got it as a reward for first place in the biology Olympiad. I just wish they weren't so cold about it," Zel said.

"Machines do all the work. That's why their—and every selection process—is so cold. That's why everything is so cold. AI runs it all. On one side, it removes human error and bias from the equation, it provides the same standards for everyone. But, it also removes human emotion, and that can be a powerful tool to receiving chances you normally wouldn't," Koa said. The conversation made Zel too anxious to continue, but she also didn't want to be rude and demand a change of topic.

Nervous, she stole a glance at Socks alone on the balcony, sitting on top of a table. Perhaps she should check on him. He didn't need to be all alone when everyone else had fun, and she wanted an excuse to leave the conversation, anyway. She politely excused herself from Koa and Vih.

Socks perched on the table, a makeshift art studio with a view. Sketches sprawled across the smooth plastic surface, anchored by a solitary burger. His gaze wandered over the cityscape, his pen capturing every detail. Yet, beneath the calm, thoughts of revenge gnawed at him.

"Socks?" Zel's voice pierced the silence, pulling him from his reverie.

He gathered his sketches as she approached, settling

into a bright yellow chair.

"I came to invite you to join us. We are having fun and...Where'd you find all this paper?" Zel asked.

"Kids' corner. They don't need it for their 'art,' " Socks said, gesturing to the deserted area with disdain. "They had a ball pit, slides, VR... and paper. Not anymore."

"Mind if I look?" Zel asked, undeterred by his brusque manner.

Socks shrugged, allowing her to peruse his sketches. Each page showed a different facet of his talent—portraits of Zel, Koa, Vih, and more. Many portraits of himself, too. In fact, those made the bulk of his gestural sketches. What Zel found interesting was, in most of them, he had given himself a train of glamorous peafowl feathers. In the sea of sketches, one stood out, depicting five demons in their true forms, united.

"Are these your friends?" Zel asked, pointing to the figures.

Socks nodded, a bittersweet smile tugging at his lips. "We didn't fit anywhere else."

"Is this you?" She pointed to the demon with silk draping over his horns. Socks rolled his eyes, laughed, then pointed to the one beside that one.

"This is me," he said, then his expression turned sad. "Remember the Tosa Inu?" Socks asked.

Zel nodded, and she pictured the muscular, imposing-looking dog with drooping jowls.

"That's my friend. The one dressed in fineries. His name is Castan. Yes, the one we saw," Socks said, pointing to the demon in the middle with a claw. "Except he didn't recognize me. He wasn't shocked or surprised or... anything. Maybe he was just not trying to let his emotions impede his work. But I'd hoped he would at least say something or come to talk to me in secret," Socks said, disappointment tinting his voice.

Zel said nothing.

"It's surprising we're even friends. Us pride demons have the strictest rankings. It's hard to mingle. Castan ranks way above me, yet never required me to bow before addressing him or the other formalities that should create an abyss between us.... One time, he used his status to remind me of my place, but that happened only once. I hate to admit it... but I was wrong, and deserved it," Socks said.

Zel could tell he was lost in fond memories, despite describing a not so great one.

"At least it answers my age-long question: Can he shoot pepper spray? And the answer is, yes, he can," Socks said, trying to smile.

"Wow. I thought you were straightforward with your powers. Why the secretiveness?" Zel asked.

Socks sighed. "It may not be true. I heard Castan once got into a fight with an envy demon. A team leader, not the one in his group. He tried to get an advantage by shooting the envy demon with pepper spray, which his opponent did not like. Then, when Castan lost the skirmish, his snout got forced against the corner of a wall, breaking his double fangs and hindering his ability to shoot it. I'd heard that it healed, but it's the first time I saw him using it. He did a shoddy job. But hey, maybe he recognized me and missed on purpose."

Zel was horrified, and her expression mirrored it. She was sure that had to count as mutilation. But demons had different laws than humans. Still horrifying. She was incredulous at Socks's trivial remark. The envy demon's reaction had been cruel and unnecessary.

"What about you? Why are you so secretive about your powers?" she asked, though she was a little afraid to. Socks's face fell again.

Please don't tell me that breaking a pride demon's fangs on a wall is a standard thing, and that happened to you, too.

94

Socks chuckled, his laughter muffled. "Envy familiars do things like that... but not that extreme. We're much stronger and faster, natural-born fighters, but in the rare case we lose, they'll force the loser to use their powers on themselves. The most common method is to take one's venomous tail barb and stab its owner with it. I've always been warned not to pick fights with them. But no, that's not my case."

Zel found it hard to believe that Socks's kind would take that advice seriously, given their inflated sense of self-importance. "Do they listen?" she asked.

"Eventually," Socks said vaguely, waving a dismissive paw. Zel furrowed her brows, perplexed.

"Hm. So what's up with your powers?" she asked.

"There's a balance in Hell," Socks said.

"What?" Zel arched a brow in confusion. "What does that have to do with anything?"

"Or at least, there was balance, before you humans threw it all off," Socks continued.

"We, what?" Zel was completely bewildered. "This conversation makes no sense."

"Before that happened, covet demons searched for lost abilities that some dubious sources claimed their ancestral kind had," Socks elaborated. "Envy demons were born without wings; they later gained them but lacked inherent powers. Besides possessing the best qualities of all others, every single pride demon also had powers. Wrath... I've offered sufficient examples to support my contention. Three will do."

Zel found it amusing how Socks's giant ears flopped every time he spoke.

"Then comes our mutual existence. Your universe has no magic. But somehow, after our species began this symbiotic relationship, non-existent human enchantment flooded Hell, and everything changed. First, part of Hell froze and remains frosty to this day. Second, some covet demons are born with abilities their ancestors had. Some envy demons gained powers. And some pride demons are born without abilities. No one knows why, what, or how. It seems to do good for all demon kinds except mine. I never understood that. I think it's because you hate all of us," Socks said.

Zel didn't understand why he had decided to have the conversation then, of all times. There was silence, interrupted only by the distant engines of AeroCars. Zel recalled the earlier situation.

"You're saying you're powerless?" Zel asked.

"Don't be blunt!" Socks growled, his eyes glowing purple, attracting the attention of several diners nearby.

"Sorry. I thought you were open to talking about it since you mentioned it," Zel apologized, realizing she'd touched a sore spot.

"Of all things your magic could have messed up, it chose the most painful for us, while every other species gets it better. Makes no sense," Socks lamented.

Zel offered him a few consolation pets, but she stopped when she noticed his sideways glance. The two stood in silence for a moment.

"Hey. Sorry for asking. Why does it bother you so much that others have powers?"

Socks's eyes were back to purple, but he said nothing.

"Are you envious?"

"It's not envy," Socks snapped. "It's... something else." He didn't specify what, though. Zel stood there in silence.

They stayed quiet for so long she considered going inside when he spoke. "They mocked me for it. Everyone. Even my friends. It was like I walked in and everything turned into a mean-spirited pity party. And they called it teasing. Or joking. Or being playful." Hints of purple sparks glinted on his pupils.

The depths of Zel's consciousness sparked burning

rage, fear of rejection, and general insecurity about things she couldn't ever change. She was sure those weren't her feelings, but Socks's, seeping through the faults in their mental link and reaching her.

"And they considered it normal. Few experiences are more disheartening than arriving at a sporting event with colleagues, only to receive pitying glances because you cannot play, or because you lack in the stature and won't do well in races or mock fights. Or on everything else, because everyone else is better than you." Socks stomped his front paws and emitted a bright purple light from his eyes that flashed white before subsiding.

"If I complain, they say I can't take a joke and am a bad sport."

Socks had had fantastic friends back where he was from. They would accompany him on things they didn't enjoy doing, but Socks did, such as markets and art galleries. They also defended him in altercations in his absence. He reciprocated their loyalty. However, his companions made unkind remarks about his lack of innate abilities or his stature, which left him feeling self-conscious and inferior. He'd often spend hours scrutinizing passersby, searching for individuals shorter than him, or attempting to convince himself the absence of powers wasn't a significant issue.

"Jokes on them. I handle loss just fine. It's not like us pride demons are sore losers or anything, despite what you humans think," Socks scoffed.

"And how do you handle it?" Zel asked, skeptical due to being familiar with his kind's tendencies, but willing to give him the benefit of the doubt.

"By throwing a fit, obviously," Socks said.

Zel's raised eyebrows made him clarify.

"But hey, I usually leave before things get ugly. That's good sportsmanship, right?" Socks added, trying to mask his discomfort.

"Sure," Zel said, holding in a laugh.

"But I try to avoid talking about it; I only mention it when I have to," Socks added.

"Do you feel out of place among your own kind?" Zel asked. She hoped he didn't think she was nosy. She felt that way among those from her home country, and she wanted to know if he did, too. Seemed like he did.

"I don't like hanging out with other pride demons. They aren't my first choice of companions. It's odd. I've noticed the same familiars clustering together at rescue centers—covet demons here, greed demons there. But not me... Most of my closest friends were wrath demons. It's ironic, considering they're at odds with us," Socks explained.

"Don't wrath demons wage war on everything? Even trees and rocks?" Zel asked, trying to wrap her head around the dynamics of demon society.

Socks chuckled. "And peace summits, too. They're banned from diplomatic missions in Hell."

Zel couldn't help but laugh, though the thought of a war instigated by wrath demons was chilling.

"Socks, why do you think you don't fit in with others like you? Is it just because of the powers?" she pressed, sensing there was more to his story.

Socks's smile faded, replaced by a somber expression. "They can be... cruel. They're mean-spirited, their jokes sting, and their jabs at powerless demons like me hurt," he admitted, his vulnerability catching Zel off guard.

She recalled past conversations with Socks, where his remarks bordered on insensitivity. But instead of pointing it out, she listened, grateful for the opportunity to understand him better. Maybe she had judged his kind too harshly. Well. They were still obnoxious and self-centered, but seemed loyal, and what she thought was deliberate, cruel mockery seemed more and more like genuine mistakes made while expressing themselves. It didn't excuse their rudeness, but it differed from if they did it on purpose. If you were in line, and someone stepped on your foot by accident, then apologized, you'd see them differently than if you knew they stepped on purpose, despite getting hurt either way.

"I will admit I am missing some... important context here. Mainly, why you seek revenge. It may not be my place to say this. But what about forgiving?" Zel asked.

"There's no point in doing so. Forgiveness lets the other party know you don't care about they did and that they can do it again," Socks snarled, causing a few guests to look.

"Hmm," Zel said.

If he didn't feel like forgiving, he had his reasons—like she had hers regarding Vih—she wouldn't insist. It is his choice to make. Zel felt like it would be best to change the subject. She opened her purse and got a little booklet with an outline of Earth, and a drawing of a jaguar stepping through coffee stalks.

"That's my passport. It's from Snil, Earth. It has the old coat of arms. A rarity."

"Earth? You are pretty far here on Venus," Socks said.

"Like every other country on Earth, air quality in Snil is not great and the once pristine rivers are overflowing with waste from centuries of exploitation. However, it remains a wonderful place, boasting great beaches, an amazing climate, and some of the best food. It's not developed and public transport is inadequate. Education is subpar, with those in power exploiting taxpayers' funds. Snilians loathe me when I bring this up, even if many of them are immigrants like me. They say everywhere has problems and I should be grateful for where I was born. I am, but they're blind to the issues in their own country." Zel paused.

"It got to where many of them asked me if I was even

a Snilian or just someone who spoke their language. Here. look at this," Zel said, whipping out her phone, and opening a bright-colored social media page. The top banner of it read "Snilians in Vivian" She scrolled down, but all the pages had a lock with a caption saying she couldn't access the page.

"I got banned from this support group, and many others, by extension. People claimed I wasn't Snilian and didn't belong there. So, I shared an update, holding up my passport to prove them wrong. I can't explain why I thought that would work."

Zel showed Socks a screenshot of a social media page. It featured her passport close to her face. The title of the post was three words he had assumed Zel didn't know. The comments were all that one would expect from such sites:

"Fake. Images can be edited to perfection. Admit it. You have poor grammar, don't give two importances for our culture. You don't even behave like one of us."

"She expects us to believe a picture, a PICTURE, despite all the software and AIs that can make those to model."

"That's one of the poorest image editing ever. That's not how our seal looks. Did you draw that piece of manure yourself?"

"I hope this clown gets permanently banned. Serves her right to impersonate us We struggle so much, then this absolute buffoon says our country sucks and shames people for going back. I bet she's a native and has never had to struggle with half the things we do."

"She isn't the only one shaming group members for returning. Plenty of us do that too. About her being from here... Yeah, lots of evidence points to that."

"Don't you all worry. We, the mod team, are well aware this image is fake. We will ban the poster soon enough and check the other affiliate groups."

"I've shamed no one for wanting to return home. I see several posts on social media from Snilians saying they're returning earlier because they can't stand it here or they're not achieving anything, and I tell them some benefits of staying if they haven't completed their courses yet. But I don't tell them to stay if they don't want to; there are plenty of other countries out there they could try." Zel sighed.

They stood in silence for a few moments. Socks had never, ever imagined Zel might understand him. She didn't act like she did. But she was well aware of the exclusion and otherness that plagued him. Zel considered how she may have judged his kind—or, to be more precise, him, who was quite different from other pride demons—harshly. In the end, he wanted acceptance and understanding, just like she did.

"Hey, Socks. I hope you don't carry out your revenge... Not because whoever it is doesn't deserve it, but because you have a heart and I can tell you you'll feel guilty for life. At least, that's what happened to me. The feeling of justice faded quite fast, and I just cried for being a terrible person. You don't need to forgive, nor should you if it was that bad, but you shouldn't hurt someone because they hurt you."

He said nothing.

Zel sighed. "We're having fun, eating, and playing in the VR holodeck. Koa is going for the dance revolution record," she said, glancing back at the restaurant where Koa, Star, and Vih were gathered, enjoying themselves as they jumped between platforms. "I came here to invite you to join us."

As they returned to the crowded restaurant, he couldn't help but feel a sense of connection with Zel.

CHAPTER 15

The otherworldly pale blue light of Venus' ice moon bathed Vih's flat, casting elongated shadows across the cluttered shelves and tables. Spark sat at the window, her gaze fixed upon the celestial spectacle above.

She lifted her snout toward the moon with a mournful howl, her plaintive cry echoing in the quiet room. Chili, occupied with perusing the bookshelves, cast a concerned glance at her canine companion, fearing Spark might topple over from her enthusiastic arching. Chili glanced at a digital clock, noting the late hour.

"So, Chili, I bent to your annoying requests to lead, and it landed us in an apartment that resulted in nothing but work. Will you obey me now?" Castan asked.

"No! Things just went wrong... But it's a marvelous plan! It would have worked if things just happened as they should, and there is no sign of the group we're chasing yet. I doubt they'll spend the night here, but if they did, we would have gotten them and my plan would have been great!" she said, her eyes scanning the room.

"Or perhaps we've got the wrong flat, and we would have them already if we kept tracking them, as I suggested, and waited for them to fall asleep before making a move. But you don't listen," Castan chimed from the couch, lounging with crossed front paws.

Chili shook her head, her senses attuned to the magical aura lingering in the room. "No mistake. I can smell it," she said, her nose lifted to catch the faintest trace of magic.

"He sat next to where you are," Chili said and pointed to the wall adorned with several pictures. "See that? We saw those girls today. At least one of them lives here," she explained, her gaze flitting between the videos of a wild-haired girl dressed in robes with a weird square hat receiving a rolled paper, the same girl, and one with very curly hair, sitting on a picnic table, laughing, and one included a very bored familiar with mismatched horns, sighing in the quiet surroundings.

Spark howled again, Chili empathizing with her companion's longing for power and purpose, recalling her own nights of frustration. Determined to focus on her task, Chili turned her attention back to the shelves to quell the rising emotions. Things had changed less than she thought it would. Everyone still ignored her, and nobody believed she could do things right. Chili focused on the books, trying to not get distracted by thoughts of unfairness. She had cried enough already. No more time for that.

"This human's got quite the collection of tomes on demon magic. Gotta appreciate her curiosity," Chili said, pulling a book out, opening it, and perusing the table of contents.

"You call it curiosity. I call it being nosy. Those who think they can manipulate our magic have poor taste. They're supposed to stop exploiting our resources. Humans ravaged their original planet by doing that. They're wrecking our realm too," Castan spat.

Chili glared at him, then closed the book in one swift move. She put it back on the shelf. She had never thought she would hear pure ignorance from her colleagues. "Magic belongs to us. Like their souls belong to them. We choose to share it. As they share their souls. They aren't exploiting us. We give them our magic because we want to. You should know demons in the human realm have free will," she said.

Spark's howls persisted. Castan placed a nearby pillow on top of his ears, his discomfort clear. "You want to lead, so go tell your subordinate to shut up," Castan said.

"Do her cries bother you?" Chili asked, jumping on the couch and lying down beside the Tosa. She would never do something like that. Spark needed the release, and she understood it. Castan used to, too.

"They do," Castan admitted, moving to the far edge of the couch.

"Hmm, our deep yearning can be quite the puzzle to unravel. But what happened to your understanding? You used to do that when your fangs were healing," Chili said.

Castan looked surprised, like he wasn't aware of that fact. "Pride demons do not do that," Castan said, pointing at Spark, who, at that exact moment, leaned too far back mid-howl and fell over, taking a moment to right themselves again.

Chili was about to make a snarky comment when her magical tablet lit up, signaling an incoming call. She sighed. "I need to unmute this thing," she muttered, answering it.

"Hello?"

"Hi, Chili. Would you be so kind as to activate the illusions?" It was her boss, the greed demon. Chili nearly dropped the tablet. She muted the call quickly.

"Spark! Get over here! Open a portal to Hell so Castan can transform before—" Chili stopped mid-sentence and magic smoke billowed from her tablet, forming the illusion of the greed demon. The boss looked exceptionally grumpy. Chili and Castan bowed immediately.

"Now unmute me," the greed demon commanded.

Chili complied.

"What a cute little bloodhound you make. You think you're so clever, hiding the fact that you're pulling the strings? Many envy demons have tried before you. They all think they can do better if they are in charge. When they get caught, we usually straighten them out with this." The greed demon held up a torturous device, making Chili wince. "But its effects are temporary. Soon enough, you're all back to coveting your superiors' jobs. So, I'm trying something different. Congratulations, you're promoted."

"What?" Chili wrinkled her nose in confusion.

"Yes, promoted. But now you're responsible for all of Castan's duties and his subordinates' as well... Spark's too,"

"What? You can't do that!" Chili said.

"You can't. I have no subordinates!" Spark chimed.

The boss gave them a long look. "You do now, Spark." She turned to Chili. "If any of them mess up, you'll answer for it. And given your track record..." the greed demon displayed the graph with the steep drop. "I don't think it will be long before there's another mistake. Since you're in charge, you alone will answer for it. Remember, some of your underlings are itching to see you fail. It's in your best interest not to give them that chance. I expect an update tomorrow." The smoke dissipated as the call ended.

Chili stared into space, her heart pounding. Fear gripped her. She didn't want that. She never coveted Castan's position. Chili just thought she could lead better. Spark's howling had stopped, and the golden retriever sat beside her.

"Chili, are you alright?" Spark asked.

"Yes, I just... need a break. See you soon." Chili bolted out of the flat, heading toward the communal kitchen.

Once she was far enough away, in a secluded corridor she thought her friends wouldn't see her weakness, she let a few tears fall. There was so much that could go wrong. So many things to manage, details to sort out, and she couldn't afford to get caught up in it all. Chili stayed there for quite some time until her tears dried and she calmed down.

Once back at unit 72's door, Chili had a suspicion and sniffed the floor. Zel's scent continued down the corridor. But no scent of Socks. She followed her nose a few doors down. Chili looked at the door. She could smell another human—different from the girl—and a familiar inside. It was quite curious.

CHAPTER 16

Harper sat in the quiet sanctuary of his room within a rescue center, not the same one Socks had lived in, in a separate wing from the plaza full of humans and their ceaseless requests for attuning. Angels did not attune, end of the story.

Harper's room was pretty much a kitchen. It had an electric stove top with a boiling pot on it. Torture devices in weird shapes sat next to the egg scrambler, ladles, and a device that looked like two strainer ladles put together so, once closed, formed a sphere that Harper called a scooper. He didn't know its name. They sold it both as a "hamster clip" or as a fancy multipurpose egg whisk. Harper eyed a multi chambered cereal dispenser. but instead of grains, the compartments held souls, sorted by color. He twisted the handle and grabbed a blue soul, then placed it in the merged strainer ladles with his talons.

Harper lowered the device into the boiling pot of demonic spices. The soul screamed. Good thing souls are almost immortal. Boiling one wouldn't end it.

Harper's smartwatch rang. Using a talon and wing, he held it to his ear. "Yes?" he said politely. His expression turned to anger at what the person on the other end said.

"What do you mean 'she's gone'? I was very clear—'no harm unless she resists.' " He stopped as the demon on the other side spoke.

Relief crossed his features, though his anger remained. "Thanks for clarifying that 'gone' means 'missing' and not 'dead.' Find her. Raid nearby towns, if you must. But find her, bring her back, and chain her to the wall. Yes, I know she was already chained. Add another one! And I need the names of everyone on duty when she escaped. Yes, all of them. Including yours." After a long pause, Harper sighed, "Understood. Get it done." He ended the call, wings twitching with frustration.

He picked up a pen from the table. It danced across the pages of his diary as he wrote the names of those he'd punish harshly. Maybe the messenger could get away with a lighter punishment, but he'd still receive punishment. Harper would do it himself because he, unlike Rubicallophrys, straightened demons out on their first failure. The others were too soft. Harper didn't hold back for anyone, not even Dryas, his then-friend. Though, Dryas had become a better ruler for it. If anything, he owed Harper thanks for that. Once done writing, Harper stared at his diary.

All he needed was to figure out the right way to remove the soul essence. That was why he had souls contained within flasks around him. To test out his hypothesis. To make it work. When he felt frustrated, like he was, he'd often fantasize about his glory. Of achieving his goal, and what it would mean if he did—but not for too long. Only long enough to get him hyped about it so he could forget the frustrations. He couldn't afford to get lost in fantasy. But he could think it up, and then afterward, think: what exactly do I need to do to make that fantasy a reality? How much work do I need to put in?

Then it would inspire him to try more. To try harder. To make it work. Maybe all diligent angels did that. At least, all the ones he knew did. It was their second nature.

The scratches of ink formed a tale of his thoughts and observations. He had to be close to figuring out Dryas's recipe. He had failed so many times already, changed so many things... Maybe it would finally be the one, and he would save the angels. A rhythmic beat of wings stirred him from his writing.

Harper turned to the door, and a raven with a yellow halo and disheveled feathers landed. "Hello, Rubicallophrys. How is the mission?" Harper asked.

Rubicallophrys hopped about, his movements

betraying the weariness beneath his avian guise. "Going well. But I can't keep it up for much longer. I was lucky neither Chili nor Spark noticed when I turned back into, well, me. I can't hold a shape for too long. I came here to take a break, be myself for a moment," he confessed, settling with a weary sigh.

Harper narrowed his eyes. "If the others wake up and see Castan is missing, we're going to have a problem," he said, his thoughts already racing to mitigate potential issues.

Rubicallophrys reassured him with a casual wave of his wing. "I've taken precautions. Both Chili and Spark are subdued with tranquilizer darts," he explained confidently.

Perhaps too much confidence. Depending on how long Harper's friend stayed in each form, some magic rubbed off on him, and he acted off for a little while. Harper did not like the idea of the fresh surge of confidence contributing to his friend committing a mistake.

"And I might have bad news. I saw a ghost," Rubicallophrys said.

"A ghost?" Harper echoed. There was silence, broken by the soul's screams.

"Or a zombie. Whatever you call someone who stopped being dead. A kind angel."

The mention of a ghost or zombie drew Harper's full attention, his ink-stained talons freezing over the pages of his diary. "A kind angel returned from the dead?" he echoed, disbelief etched in the lines of his face. That wasn't good.

Rubicallophrys nodded. "I saw the scars—over his heart and mirrored on his back. He bore a striking resemblance to—"

"Impossible," Harper said, his wings flaring. Memories of a desperate plan, a flight in the human world, and an unexpected issue followed by a crash surged to the forefront of his mind, ending with Dryas literally colliding with death's finality. "Dryas died. We saw it."

"If it is him, it's bad, in a way. But in another, perhaps we could get him to tell us how he collected essence the way he did. It would be way more useful than our trial and error method. How many pages are in that book? How many fails? We're running out of time, and you're not close to figuring it, are you? We could get his method. Just make sure he writes it this time," Rubicallophrys said.

"So your idea is to swoop down and talk to him?"

"More or less. Since he attuned with a human, it may have impaired his judgement. We need to test the ground first. Maybe return him to Abundance, see how he reacts, then we ask."

Harper sighed. "It's not him. Dryas would never befriend humans," he tried telling himself so it would feel true. "This will refuel your shapeshifting powers." Harper said, taking the soul from the pot and the scooper, giving it to his friend, who pinned it down with a talon.

"But if you're going to figure out where Socks hid all those human world trinkets, do it fast, or else angels will starve."

Rubicallophrys gave a grateful nod. He sapped the blue light from the soul until it stopped wiggling, but still breathed. Its sweet contents offered temporary relief from the strain.

"This tastes way better than Dryas's sweet and sour recipes," he mused. "But it's still not as rich. The soldiers have returned from another raid. They got more soul cookbooks saved from the burnings,"

"Wonderful! Be vigilant, alright?" Harper said.

"I shall be careful," he vowed and flew into the unknown.

CHAPTER 17

Meanwhile, an AeroCar with a turtle paint job sat in the parking lot of a busy 24-7 mall parking.

The AeroCar was on, its heating system keeping the car at the perfect temperature. Oxygen levels were steady. After all, it's not like the windows rolled down. A purple tint from the car being in Roadtrip mode covered the windows, allowing less sunlight to filter in so the travelers could sleep in peace or do things to end boredom without being bothered by the sunlight. Somehow, all five of them had fit, and dozed away.

As Zel drifted away, she had the same feeling from when she dreamed of Willow. She could tell she was not only dreaming about Socks, she was becoming him.

The place smelled of sulfur. Stalagmites, ranging from sequoia to grass blade sized, dotted Hell's red, rocky landscape. Geysers spewed black smoke at regular intervals. Hot wind rattled Socks's wings as he flew in his true form—hooves, tusks, thick scales. Fear engulfed him. He readied his yelath, a demonic weapon, and was glad for his wing blades. His enemies were close.

"We're almost there. Keep flying," Harper urged, his feathered wings fluffed in terror. Around forty demons and angels, including an angel named Javabelenois, flew with them.

"But the landscape hasn't changed. We can't be near Abundance," Javabelenois argued, his orange halo dim.

"We're near a safety tower. We'll hide there," Harper said, beating his wings harder.

"I should've told my friends where I was going. They had no idea. They didn't want me trying to travel for Abundance. I wanted to bring them with me, but I came to check it myself first. How reckless of me," Javabelenois said, as he flew faster and faster.

A piercing screech filled the air. Socks turned toward the sound in one swift move. He held his yelath and saw one of them. The enemy. An abomination. It glided through the air, its four bird-like wings creating small tornadoes in their wake. Its many eyes blinked in slight offset.

It dropped a demon's body. Socks couldn't fire without hitting his comrades. It wasn't the first time an abomination had gotten personal with a group he was in, but that wasn't a thing one got used to. It was scary every single time, and always would be.

The demons panicked, scattering. Socks tried to shoot. He fired quite a few times, but since the abomination still stood, he must have missed.

Another abomination appeared beside him. So close Socks saw each feather, each scale, reflected in its six eyes. It pointed what looked like a strange yelath at Socks.

Burning pain seared through Socks's right wing, and he slashed the beast's eyes with his wingblades. Socks aimed the yelath at the abomination's head, and hesitated for a split second—like he always did. He knew the abomination was someone's friend. Someone's family. He didn't want to do it. Doing it never got easier. But that thing had ended the lives of dozens, if not hundreds, of his kind. If he didn't do it, it would end many, many more. He fired. It fell silent, plummeting to the rocks below

Only then did Socks realize he was losing altitude at an alarming speed. His right wing wasn't working properly. He beat his wings in a mismatched pattern, hoping to ease his fall. A third abomination soared over him. It had Javabelenois's corpse impaled on a spear.

Socks flew like a fly without its halters. Fast and with no idea of where he was going. He only had two things on his mind: don't get eaten, and don't crash into one of those huge stalagmites at this speed.

Several shots echoed behind him. Some distant, others not so much. His hooves reached the stone floor. He started running. Socks was bleeding quite a lot. He needed a tourniquet. He rummaged his belt for one, found it, and tied it on his right wing. The thing was so tight he felt it would cut his wing clean off.

"Latalaeumaeus, over here!" Harper shouted from the safety tower entrance.

Socks ran, bleeding, and somehow made it inside. The doors closed behind him, sealing out the chaos.

Twenty demons and angels huddled inside the tower, lit by magic lights. Harper sat beside Socks. "We can reach the city through these towers," he said.

"I need a hospital in less than two hours," Socks muttered. He looked, but he didn't see. His brain wasn't processing things right. He saw demons, but he didn't really see them. His mind focused elsewhere.

"We should be safe here. Let's wait and see if anyone else makes it. Our collective angelic magic is fading. We're starving. If we don't get proper nutrition soon, they'll invade our cities," Harper said.

Unless the tower's magic falters, Socks thought, but didn't say.

"I was waiting till we got to Abundance. But you seem in need of a distraction. Here are your human world trinkets." Harper said, handing Socks a bag full of human world magazines and print media.

Socks conjured a paper for demonic deals out of thin air and handed it to Harper. That was the deal. Harper would bring human-world media for Socks, and Socks provided the Harper with demonic papers and magic items Socks knew were being unlawfully smuggled to the human world and sold in the smuggler's market, but preferred to turn a blind eye to. He never gave Harper dangerous goods. One of the magazines had

113

a bookmark. But Socks had been too aloof to notice it.

But Zel did. She was herself for a moment and remembered her mom showing her the magazine. Then Zel was back to being Socks, who grabbed a booklet sticking out of the bag.

He flipped through it, longing for the peaceful scenes depicted within.

"Latest edition," Harper commented, glancing at the media Socks held.

"How was the trip to the human world?" Socks asked, scanning through the pages of buildings and furniture. He would draw them later.

"The same. I check if things are under control, bring back leftovers from the attuning..." Harper trailed off. "What about your job at Silverworks?"

"Same as always. Lots of silver, lava, and screaming," Socks said, flipping through the pages. The little demon dogs looked so happy in them, away from all the war nonsense going on in Hell. Socks felt a strong urge to be in the picture.

Socks pointed out a feature on LED screens in the human world, pondering how they powered them. Harper expressed interest, peering at the magazine, only to discover that Socks had mistaken the sky for a giant television.

Screams and roars echoed outside. Two bloodied demons stumbled in. One had a mauled wing, the other was covered in her friend's blood.

"Will I ever go there?" Socks asked, staring at the magazine.

"To the human world? That's anyone's guess," Harper replied.

"I hate this place. All the death, war. I feel worthless. I need to leave before they assign me to the front lines," Socks said. "Who cares if a silverworks soldier leaves? No one! All we do is silver brand human world demons accepted to stay there forever," Socks admitted. His wing hurt more, and he felt woozy. The adrenaline was wearing off.

"Wanting is dangerous. It leads to free will," Harper warned.

"I already have it," Socks retorted.

Harper panicked, flaring his wings and jumping back. "How did you develop it with no humans around?"

Socks glanced at the magazines. Harper did too. "Give me those back! They're not helping you," Harper said, reaching for them. Socks didn't let him take them.

"We had a deal," Socks declared. "I'll leave this place. Even if I have to silver brand myself."

The memory faded to a blur of days. Even weeks. Huge sums of money exchanged hands. Interviews were made. Bureaucracy got in the way. But then, they solved it all... in a way. Then another memory snapped into focus. Socks held down by two bulky constructs powered by a magic charge. But he was there willingly. He could ask them to let him go. In front of him stood a demon dressed in armor, wearing thick gloves, holding a silver branding iron to heat it over lava. The brand trembled in the hands of Socks's best friend, Castan.

"You are really lucky. Very few demons get to go to the human world with the silver brand of permanent residency," Castan said as he heated the rod.

"As long as no one finds out what we're doing..." Socks scoffed, then noticed his friend had moved the rod away from the lava. Its color was lighter than before, but it wasn't hot enough. "The brand must be glowing yellow."

Castan paled a little, but returned the brand to the lava. "It will be fine," Castan said, removing the now yellow brand from the lava.

"Fifteen seconds, Castan. Fifteen seconds. Not less, and definitely not more," Socks said. He knew his friend couldn't endure his screams that long. The construct held

Socks palm open. Castan touched the brand on it. For exactly eight seconds.

CHAPTER 18

The morning sun bathed the AeroCar, casting light on the sleepy faces of the humans and their familiars nestled in small baskets.

Zel woke with a jolt. She gasped and checked her palms. A wave of relief washed over her once she noticed she wasn't branded.

Memory dreams were weird. She hoped to never have another one again.

"Are you alright?" Socks asked, placing his front paws on the side of the basket to have a better view.

"Yes... I... May I check your silver brand?" she asked.

Socks placed a paw in her hand. She eyed the scar. *Luma's is deeper... These hurt so much... Why don't demons find a better way?* Zel thought.

"I had a memory dream... of when you got branded..." Zel said, letting go of his paw. "Yours is a forgery, isn't it? That's why the razorbacks are chasing you. At first, it confused me... I didn't understand why you couldn't stay."

"Forgery is a strong word..." Socks said. "I had a memory dream too. You were quite young and found some leather clothes and a whip in your mom's wardrobe and thought she was secretly a superhero."

Zel blushed. "Yes... I did... But today I know it is just cosplay, even if I find it a tad exposed."

Socks blinked at her. Quite a few times.

"If you say so," he said. Zel rolled her eyes. Socks couldn't possibly believe her mom was an actual superhero, right? She stretched and recoiled when she kicked someone.

"Oops. Sorry, Koa. Are you awake?" she asked.

"I am since I got that foot to the face," they said, sitting up and petting Star, who curled up in a basket in front of their seat with care.

"Wake up..." they said, causing Star to blink and stretch.

Zel checked her smart watch. That woke her up for real. "Eleven thirty? Aren't we meant to be somewhere by noon?"

"Don't worry. It isn't far..." Vih said, not bothering to get up. "Get ADAN working and I'll input the address. Wake me up when we get there," she yawned.

Shortly after, the turtle AeroCar parked in front of a store adorned with neon signs and a giant burger on the roof. Inside, the self-order kiosks sported long queues, while hovering rectangular robots with long arms efficiently cleared trays left by customers.

Socks, Star, their humans, and Vih sat across from Hawke and two serious-looking silver ravens with gleaming metal helmets. Hawke pecked at a pile of french fries on the table.

"So... We're waiting," Zel said, smiling politely.

The golden raven raised her gaze. "You left me waiting, too," Hawke said, returning to her food.

"We're very sorry. Please?" Vih pleaded. Hawke rolled her eyes and gestured to the nearest raven, who placed the ornamental box holding the Heart Stone on the table.

"The price is soul essence, as much as each of you can give," Hawke explained. Socks looked impressed. The humans shared a surprised glance.

"What?" Koa exclaimed, outraged, slamming the table. "No! You aren't taking my soul. I draw the line here, Zel. I won't give you a piece of myself."

Star stretched a paw to calm them.

"Zel... uh... We are friends and all... But uh... I don't.... erm... think they would find my essence acceptable. So it's a no from me," Vih said.

Zel understood that, too.

"Because your soul tastes bad?" Socks asked, skeptical.

"Yes... terrible. Take my word for it," Vih said.

"Hawke, that's... uh... a tad... above my budget. Perhaps we could... haggle a little?" Zel asked. There had to be something else she'd accept, right?

The two soldiers looked at Hawke. Zel couldn't tell much from their stoic raven faces, but Socks could. They threatened Hawke with that look. She had promised them something, and they were there to collect.

"Hmm... I suppose I could settle for the essence of a single soul," she said. The ravens looked back at Zel with their intense white eyes.

"I... erm..." Zel said. She should have worded that better. She had forgotten demons were known for trickery like that.

"Dear, those raven's helmets bear Abundance's insignia. I gather the city still stands. Who rules it?" Star asked, his tail wagging.

It was an obvious attempt at breaking the tension. Socks eyed the ravens, noting the tree coat of arms on their helmets. The ravens looked a tad puzzled, even worried. The greed demon was quite surprised herself.

"Look it up if you don't know," Hawke dismissed Star's inquiry, focusing on the task at hand. The blue dog looked at his paws, saddened.

"About the soul essence... I hope you're willing to trade it. Have you made up your mind? Souls replenish over time. You won't miss just a little, will you?" the golden raven asked.

"Erm... does it hurt?" Zel asked.

"A little," Hawke said.

"It's way more than a little. Giving soul essence has been likened to—" Vih started, then the golden raven jumped at her face.

"Silence!" Hawke called, making Vih flinch. Then she must have felt bad, because she softened a little and looked a tad guilty. "You are... Scaring your friend,"

"But I should know the truth, shouldn't I?" Zel asked. No one answered. She guessed that meant "no." Or that they were afraid of Hawke. She stood in silence.

A drone carrying colorful trays flew behind them, reminding Zel of the warm atmosphere of the restaurant.

She looked at Socks. "What do you think?" she asked.

He rubbed his chin. *Well. I don't want to be executed by a volcano, nor do I want to explode out of existence. I want you to do it. But I can't tell you that. It is your soul. It is up to you. I don't think I can tell you that without guilting you into doing something you don't want to. But again, may I remind you what you do want, which is a familiar that's not me, but that sounds like a jerk move, too... Maybe I should just... Wait. Zel? Is this you? Are you listening? Stop listening to my thoughts! What have you heard? Oh, Malah!*

After cursing in Demon, Socks walled off his thoughts. He had been right. Hearing that made her feel a little bad for at least not considering it.

"I can't make that decision for you. If anything, I'd tell you to not do it. Inexperienced demons and angels, which we all are due, no one learning to manipulate souls since attuning started, can take too much and kill the soul by accident," Socks said.

Zel paled. The thought of death made her reconsider. It wasn't worth it. She could study elsewhere, and hopefully they'd find a safer way to unattune.

"Don't scare her. Inexperience may cause... accidents. But don't worry, the one who will take your essence is anything but," Hawke said as the soldiers moved.

Zel felt uneasy at the thought of unfamiliar angels handling her soul.

Socks leaped onto the table, baring his teeth to intimidate them. It worked, and the soldiers hesitated. Perhaps they feared he had venom. "From Abundance or not,

I wouldn't trust them to do it. They're angels. They're always half starved. And they might slip and take too much. Besides, wasn't there a story about Abundance not using real souls?"

"I wasn't referring to them, but to your blue friend over there," Hawke said, ignoring the last line. Everyone stared at Star, who closed his eyes and took a deep breath.

"Why me?" he asked.

"Because it is obvious, you are—" Socks said before Zel silenced him.

If Star wanted them to know, he would've told them. They shouldn't spill his secret.

"...Good at it,"

"So, decide soon. My companions are losing patience and we don't want that to happen, right?" Hawke asked.

There was a hint of nervousness in her voice. Was she in trouble, and by extension, was Zel and her friends too? Zel's heart raced. The soldiers looked grumpy.

To hopefully save Socks from a horrible fate, and for my academic future!

"I will do it. Yes, I am sure. Be quick before I change my mind.," Zel said as she trembled a little.

Star climbed onto the table. "Are you really sure?" Star asked.

"Yes," she said.

Socks spit out her soul, but before Star could reach for it, Socks intervened.

"Hurt her longer than what's needed and I'll smash your face in," Socks threatened, his eyes narrowed.

Socks's protectiveness surprised Zel, even if she didn't condone his aggressive approach. *Maybe he does like me...* she thought.

Star looked concerned, glancing at Koa, who seemed too bored to react. "Let's, uh... give her something to hold," Vih said.

Koa muttered something, then typed on their smartwatch. Their neural interface flashed blue, and so did the screen of a nearby food delivery robot. Koa then grabbed an orange from the fruit on its tray and handed it to Zel, who held it in her left hand. The drone flew away, not noticing it was missing something. Koa really knew their stuff.

"Uh... Thanks, I guess," Zel said, eyeing the fruit, supposing it was better than nothing.

"I'll be careful," the blue dog assured. Socks lowered the soul toward him.

Hello, and I am sorry, Zel heard in her... not mind, but soul. It was Star. He looked at the light tadpole and sank his claws into it.

Zel shivered and felt like icicles had jammed into her sides. She didn't know what Star did next, only saw a flourish that didn't even seem to touch her soul.

Zel winced and crushed the orange, spraying the table with juice. Citrus assaulted the group's sense of smell as droplets created sticky spots wherever they landed.

It hurt. A lot. Like being struck by lightning, though she had never been, she was sure the experience would be similar. It felt a little like getting blood drawn, and a weird feeling spread as Star extracted the magic, forming it into an orb. As Star continued, Zel felt an increasing fatigue, struggling to keep her posture. It was like he was taking something she'd never get back. A cold, numb feeling spread over her, overtaking the pain.

"Stop! You took way too much already!" Zel pleaded, panting.

"No, I didn't. The—" Star never finished his sentence, Socks clocked him over the head. Zel felt a smidge of sympathy for him, but again, a demon's horns and thick skull intended for bashing at flight speeds meant he was fine.

"You don't get to decide when someone else has had

enough! Stop it!" Socks said.

"But the books says it's fine to—"

"Stop it or I'll make you!" Socks bared his teeth. For a moment, it looked like soldiers would intervene, but they didn't.

"I believe that is enough," Hawke said.

Star finished waving the existing magic into an orb, then handed Zel's soul back to Socks, who placed it back in his pouch with care.

"Hand it to them," Hawke instructed. Star complied, handing the soldier the shiny orb. The two ravens inspected the light, then disappeared in a flash of bright, pure light.

Zel couldn't stop panting. She realized she had a wet, sticky thing in her left hand. She looked. It was the orange, a gooey mess. *Never again*, she thought.

Hawke slid the Heart Stone box toward Zel with a talon. Then, a few napkins too. Zel opened it to verify its authenticity, finding the glowing rock inside. "Thanks, Hawke," she said, stifling a yawn, and she cleaned her hand.

"You're welcome. Go. I will finish my lunch," Hawke dismissed. The group got up from the table and headed for the doors. Zel looked at the Heart Stone.

"Can't believe we did it," she said.

"We just broke at least a hundred laws, and you gave your soul away, no biggie," Koa said, folding their arms as the group pushed through the crowd and stopped to allow hovering drones carrying trays to fly past.

"Stop scaring her. She didn't. Essence is like a soul's blood. She'll be fine, and the soul is too," Vih said. That helped Zel relax a little.

"Hey... I'm hungry. How about we eat something?" Vih suggested.

Zel's stomach rumbled, but she knew her bank account wouldn't appreciate eating out twice in a row.

CHAPTER 19

Chili observed as Castan led them through a busy street, AeroCars hummed above and groups of kids navigated the world on flying bikes. She was trying to learn what exactly made him commit no mistakes and receive respect so she could copy it. But nothing out of the ordinary stood out to her. She didn't want to lead... not in the sudden "succeed or we will break you" way they imposed on her.

Chili couldn't help but notice the vibrant graffiti adorning a towering wall as they arrived at an intersection.

"We're here," Castan declared, facing his colleagues.

"Where are we?" Chili asked, scanning the busy street. "I still think we should have followed my plan, invaded that second apartment, and tied the people there up! It was a wonderful idea! We should be there, not here. I can't believe you prevented us from doing that to drag us to... to ...." She had no idea where she was.

"A Trashmart," Castan said, pointing to the neon sign. Chili craned her neck to see the display windows showcasing various items. "Besides, you agreed I should lead because you're afraid of committing a mistake. It's different when we must face the consequences of our choices, isn't it?"

Chili ignored that. But yes, she was afraid. She knew Castan made things work. That was why she followed him, but she wanted others to listen to her, too.

"Why are we even here? I can't pick up our target's magical signature. We don't have time for a stroll," Chili protested.

"We're here to get you those goggles every envy demon wears, but you refuse to," Castan snapped.

"I'm not getting them. Let's go. Come on, Spark," Chili insisted, moving to cross the street until

Castan blocked her path.

"You don't understand. That's an order from your boss. You can play leader all you want, but I'm the boss. I have the ultimate say. And you're getting those goggles, like it or not," Castan asserted.

"I'm the boss now," Chili growled.

"Only when it suits you, it seems. Decide yourself. Do you want the responsibility and the consequences of it? Or no? Besides, deep down, you know you still answer to me."

Chili wanted it... somewhat. She just thought the consequences were a tad over the top. Maybe sharing her ideas wasn't worth it.

"I can handle being without them," Chili retorted.

"You don't realize how embarrassing that was. Three teens incapacitated us, a trained elite team, with a flashlight, twice. Our team is known situations like this, ones we could've avoided if you wore those goggles. You say you want is to do things by the book, so stop cherry picking the rules you do and don't follow and put on a pair of goggles," Castan argued.

"Those are optional, not a rule," Spark said.

"Questioning our competence, are we?" Chili growled.

"No, just yours. You're terrible. I should've taken control of this mission from the start. Get into that store now, or I'll punish you for insubordination," Castan threatened.

"I'd love to see you try," Chili challenged.

Castan lunged forward, but Spark intervened, jumping between them.

"Stop," Spark interjected, turning to Chili. "He's right. That was embarrassing for all of us. No need to buy anything, just look," she suggested.

"You said you were trying to learn from me. So learn by obeying!" Castan growled.

"You're not yourself today," Chili told Castan, heading toward Trashmart's sliding doors. As they entered, stacks of soft plush dog beds, shelves of fake decoration plants, and snacks like chocolate bars and bags of shiitake mushroom crisps greeted Chili. Robot drones flitted about, restocking shelves and displaying holograms of various products to shoppers.

"Excuse me," Chili said to one of the drones.

It turned to face her. "Yes?" it responded.

"Where can we find those ridiculous eye-covering things everyone's wearing these days?" Chili asked, earning a facepalm from Castan and a concerned look from Spark.

"You mean the goggles envy demons wear? We have a vast selection. Follow me," the drone said, leading them to a dimly lit corridor. Boxes filled the shelves, and a table labeled "testers" attracted familiars and their humans. Chili hated to admit it, but she could tell straight away that the lighting was kinder on her eyes.

Chili was surprised to see many envy demons willingly trying on goggles without being prompted. She'd always assumed humans forced them to wear those, but she realized it was more of a choice. Curiously, she noticed covet demons also trying them on.

"Alright, I'll wear these silly goggles, on one condition: you two will do the same," Chili said.

CHAPTER 20

A few hours later, in the quiet parking lot, Socks sat atop the AeroCar, sketching his surroundings. A paper cup filled with delicious soft cream appeared by his side.

"Thought you might enjoy it," Zel said, leaning on the AeroCar and sipping her taro milk tea, gazing at the afternoon sky.

"Are you feeling okay? Your soul has curled into a ball and hasn't moved since," Socks said.

"Just a bit cold and drained. I still can't believe we did it," Zel said.

"Eager to get the ritual going?" Socks asked, prompting Zel to reflect on him. He wasn't such an unwelcome companion, and they could brainstorm ways to repel the razorbacks and stay attuned. Maybe. She feared he'd act all obnoxious if they spent more time together.

"Hard to tell. There's something I want to tell you before we split. I've been thinking about what you said about human magic making your life worse because we hate you. Upon reflection, I don't think that's the problem," Zel said, noticing Socks's reaction.

"Go on," Socks said.

"I think magic makes it easier for you to act on your nature. For instance, the best powers, strength and stamina, can inflate one's ego. Being devoid of wings and abilities while others have them can lead to envy or longing. Human magic attempts to make acting on your nature harder. If you give covet and envy demons what they wish, they may become less envious... If you... take out what your kind believes makes you better than everyone else... You won't be so arrogant," Zel elaborated.

Socks seemed intrigued but skeptical. "Why isn't

everyone affected, then?" he asked.

"Because it wouldn't work. Envy demons wouldn't feel special if everyone had powers... Same goes for your kind, but in reverse. The goal is to show you what's wrong with your kind so you can improve it," Zel explained.

"Do you think there is something wrong with my kind?" Socks snapped.

"No!" Zel said defensively, but soon looked sheepish. "Maybe? I mean... There is something wrong with everyone, no?" she tried to save it.

"May I ask you something?" Socks asked, his voice gentle, and his gaze drifted to the crowd ahead for a moment.

"Alright," Zel said, taking a sip of her drink.

"What makes you dislike pride demons so much? Don't lie to me. I saw it in your mind. You have a very low opinion of us and merely tolerate me," Socks said.

Zel took a drink of her milk tea, taking deep, deliberate gulps, letting the cold, bold flavor distract her from the question. She wanted to keep quiet, but part of her felt like Socks deserved an explanation for her seemingly random bouts of anxiety and rudeness toward him. Not that it justified them, but it explained her mood swings.

Finally, she sighed. "Okay. It is personal. Pride demons gave me this," she said, lifting her left jacket sleeve. A scar ran from her elbow to almost her wrist, faded but darker than her natural skin tone, almost purple.

"I don't like remembering it. I still have nightmares about it," Zel admitted, her voice trembling slightly. "But... this is what happened..."

Zel held a shopping bag and sat in the AeroCar in the mall's parking lot with her mom and Luma. It was broad daylight. Zel was excited to get home and try on her new clothes when a man wearing a mirrored helmet walked in front of the car. He went straight to her mom's window and held a railgun to the glass.

"Out of the vehicle, now!" he commanded. His voice was distorted, robotic.

Fear flooded Zel. She tried to look away but froze when she saw another person with a mirrored helmet pointing a railgun at her window. Both robbers dressed to conceal any features, making it impossible for her—or the technology in her smart contact lens—to recognize them later.

"Out of the vehicle!" the robber shouted and shot the AeroCar. Zel winced.

Her mom opened the door. The three of them stepped outside. The guy pointed the railgun at her mom and the other person moved in front of Zel and aimed the weapon at her. She trembled, adrenaline coursing through her veins. She thought she'd die. A commotion revealed Luma struggling on the pavement. Zel initially thought Luma had been shot, then noticed the robbers' familiars. The one closest to Luma had a scorpion-like tail—indicating a pride demon. He had attacked Luma with that tail. The second robber had a familiar too, but Zel hadn't identified it.

"Smartwatches, now!" the robber demanded. Zel quickly took hers off. Her mom did the same. One robber snatched their watches from their hands, along with Luma's collar and their shopping bags.

"Hand over anything else!" he demanded in his distorted, robotic voice.

"That's all we have! I swear!" her mom pleaded, glancing at Luma, who was in terrible pain.

But Zel still had her school tablet in her pocket. She reached into her pocket to get it, but both weapons pointed at her.

"Hands out of your pockets!" he demanded.

She obeyed, but lifted her hand too quickly. Before she could explain she was getting her tablet to hand it over, the scorpion-tailed demon struck. His tail slashed at her arm, opening a red gash. Pain shot through her nerves. Zel's world spun. She struggled to breathe as the pain spread, and she lost touch with reality. Her mom later told her she hadn't fallen unconscious and hadn't been fully sedated, but her brain had erased those memories.

The next thing Zel remembered was waking up hours later in a hospital.

Zel looked at Socks.

He searched for the right words. What could one possibly say to things like that? "That's horrible," he said once the silence grew too large. "I'm sorry that happened to you. Those were some real donkey heads. It took courage to share that. Thanks for trusting me," Socks said, his response a blend of genuine outrage and what he had read was the proper way to react in such situations.

"What are you doing after we get things sorted out?" Zel asked, trying to change the subject as fast as possible.

"Getting my revenge. I'll make her pay for what she did to me. Then I'll hide in a hole until I figure out how to stay in the human world. What about you?" he asked.

A noise startled them, and Zel glanced over to see Koa and Vih laughing at something across the parking lot. She hoped they weren't laughing at her.

"Join the Maritime Expedition, get straight As on every subject, volunteer in lots of places, and study and prepare to join Madlen University one day. My dream is to study there."

Socks was going to say something when Zel's smartwatch played rock music.

Zel answered it and a hologram of her mom popped up. She looked grumpy.

"Zel, where have you been?" Mom's voice was sharp.

Zel froze, her eyes wide. "I told you, I was at Vih's friend's."

"Don't lie to me! I checked the address you gave me. It

132

leads to a vertical farm!"

Oh no... Koa... Why?

"Then, I received a notification that the AeroCar had been on all night!" Her mom paced. "Then I thought you'd gone off somewhere, then I realized you turned off your live location ten minutes after we talked, and I looked at ADAN'S location history and there was a massive gap! I was about to call the police! Where were you? And Vih! Wasn't she with you?"

This is bad... Zel thought. Socks kept quiet, knowing it wasn't his business to meddle in.

"Vih is fine," Zel said, filming her friend for mom to see. "We were camping, okay? In the AeroCar. A harmless adventure,"

"Harmless?" Mom's voice rose. "Sleeping in an AeroCar is not harmless! Anything could've happened! If people rob others in crowded, plain daylight, imagine what evil they'd do to lone sixteen-year-olds at night in an untraceable location! You have no idea how lucky you are to be fine!"

Her mom was right, as mothers often were. Maybe Zel and her friends should have thought that plan through better.

Zel crossed her arms "Well, if you didn't dismiss my feelings so much, I would've felt I could tell you what I was doing and why! We were safe!"

"You're sixteen! You don't get to decide what's safe! I am your mother! You must tell me everything, regardless of what you think!" her mom said.

"I'm not a child anymore! You don't trust me to make my own decisions," Zel said, her anger flaring.

Mom's face furrowed and her worry grew. "Your decisions are 'Let's sleep in an AeroCar in a secluded place'! I can't trust you if you keep doing things like that, lying, and hiding things from me! It's not about trust! It's about responsibility. What if something went wrong? What if you got hurt? What if Vih got hurt?"

"Nothing happened, Mom! You're always overreacting! And you don't react at all to the things you should!" Zel snapped.

Her mom glared. "But it could have! I'm caring about your safety! The things you want me to care about are all ridiculous, Zel! I won't panic because you failed the Maritime Expedition exam! You need someone to ground you into reality! I am that person! It doesn't matter if you pass or not! You are sixteen! Life is long! Your grandma has been in this world for 110 years! The world won't end if you don't make it to Madlen University! Don't lie to me, we don't lie to our mothers."

"Maybe if you respected my feelings and fears a little more, I wouldn't have to lie!" Zel yelled. A small silence ensued. Even Koa and Vih noticed, and they turned to face her. Her mom made a shocked face.

"Go to your room!" her mom yelled. Force of habit, most likely, because she could see Zel was in a parking lot, kilometers away from her room.

"I can't go to my room because you live in my room!" Zel yelled back and hung up. Her face flushed up.

"Zel, is everything ok?" Vih asked, approaching and leaning on the car beside her.

"I just had a fight with my mom," Zel said, then wiped her eyes with a sleeve. "Why do we argue so often?"

"You two are like old and young pride demons—each thinks they're right and won't admit they might be wrong," Socks said, then realized Zel didn't want an answer. So he approached and nuzzled her hand so she could pet him. She did.

Socks wasn't a fan of pets, but he had heard once that it made humans feel better.

"Hey, let's go to Trashmart to buy the candles for the ritual. What do you think?" Vih asked. That didn't seem that bad of an idea.

"Alright," Zel said, following her colleagues, Socks bringing up the rear.

CHAPTER 21

Chili prowled, her nose close to the carpet, her goggles catching the light as she scanned the area. In the building's corridors, she paused, taking in the vibrant vehicles that flew past the windows and the lush, plant-covered architecture that surrounded the doors on the other side. Spark, meanwhile, bounded like a deer.

"So we're returning to that blonde teen's house?" Spark asked as they passed unit 72.

"Even better. I sensed Zel's soul magic further down the corridor that night. I have a theory I would like to test."

"We don't have time for the scientific method," Castan said.

"Are you going to play boss again?" Chili teased and stopped by a door. Yes, Zel's soul had been there.

"The only one playing boss is you," Castan said.

The bloodhound narrowed her eyes.

"I can smell Zel's soul too," Spark declared.

"Let's prove to the world we aren't as incompetent as everyone says. I have an idea." Chili knocked on the door.

The door opened, revealing Zel's mom and Luma by her feet.

"Oh... Hi. Erm. How can I help?" Mom asked the ominous-looking familiars.

Chili said nothing. She just snarled and flicked a paw. Spark and Castan lunged into the unit.

CHAPTER 22

Trashmart was busy. People of all ages strolled by, hovering drones flew around, and large, slow rectangular robots moved stock from shelf to shelf.

Zel stood by the self-service check-out. She had poured all the candles into the chute and waited for the machine to scan and pack it all for her. Her smartwatch rang. It was her mom. She denied the call. Zel wanted more time before talking to and apologizing to her mom. She knew her mom was right, but she also felt she was a little right, too.

Socks trotted over, holding a packaged clipper in his mouth. He gave it to her. "Can we buy that as well?" Socks asked.

"May I know why? I think paying a dog-groomer robot is easier," Zel said.

"It's for my revenge. I was going to do it by hand, like..." He shut his eyes. "But I thought what you said about revenge being cruel and not being able to live with myself. So I decided on a less hurtful method that would cause the same result," Socks said.

Zel stared at the clippers. Socks couldn't possibly want them for their intended purpose, right? She had to talk to him about that. But probably not in a busy department store. She eyed the checkout scanner. The chute was still overflowing with candles. She didn't think it would be done anytime soon, and she didn't want to look at the price.

"How about we go get some fresh air?" she asked.

Socks nodded.

"Hey, Vih?" Zel called.

Vih looked over from the e-book section.

"Can you please keep an eye on the checkout? I am going outside with Socks."

Vih gave her a thumbs up.

Wasn't long before the two left the department store and jumped on top of the AeroCar's smooth icy surface, sat, and gazed at the skyline, the distant biodome, and several vehicle lights as a chilly wind messed their fur and hair. Above them, on the parking lot's edge, towered a giant holographic billboard with rotative ads. The current one showcased a toothpaste and cast an orange light over the pavement.

Zel's gaze softened. "I was thinking about... your revenge," she confessed.

"You say that as if we spent more than two days together." Socks's response was curt, his demeanor guarded. Zel's disappointment was plain, her shoulders slumping as she processed his words.

"Look... I... It's probably not my business, but... What is up with that? What made you so mad you want to use clippers as a torture device?" Zel asked.

"I..." Socks sighed. "You probably noticed my actions have been sheepish. Not a very pride demon-like attitude, right? I'll tell you why, so you can agree with me and buy those clippers for me."

Zel's lips twitched with a hint of a smile, her amusement tempered by the sincerity in Socks's words. "Sheepish" wouldn't be a word she'd use to describe him. Ever. It'd be like calling a turtle "short-lived." "You think you're sheepish?" she couldn't help but ask.

"No. I'm not... but I might have acted a little sheepish these last few days." Socks's response was a rare glimpse into the depths of his inner turmoil.

Zel fought to keep her composure, her laughter bubbling as she struggled to believe he thought himself sheepish.

"The first thing you asked when you saw me was 'Where are your feathers?' So did the others. Do you

140

want the answer?"

Before she could respond, Socks offered an explanation.

"That envy demon you were going to attune to happened, that's what," he said.

"You mean, Willow?" Zel asked.

"You two must've had a strong connection for her to mind speak to you without attuning," Socks said. "But maybe it's better that you didn't. She's just horrible. I did nothing to her. We never crossed paths. Fine, if it had been someone else, you might have said I deserved it as payback. Which would be wrong. But you could say it," Socks said.

Zel noticed he flicked his forked tongue more often, like when she convinced him to accept Koa's help. His expression changed as he looked at his claws. His eyes shone like beacons, his downward gaze filling the area with a purple glow.

"They were the most beautiful feathers ever. Do you know how peafowls have a train of feathers? I had one too. They sparkled in the light. I liked to flare them..."

Socks stood by the tranquil waters of the rescue center's fountain, painting, and his vibrant plumage unfurled in all its resplendent glory. His feathers shimmered with hues of green, cyan, red, orange, and yellow, a dazzling display of nature's artistry.

Socks added a touch of purple to his self-portrait. The reflection in the water mirrored his image.

A voice broke through the silence, drawing Socks's attention to the figure approaching him. Willow, with her vibrant red fur and piercing green eyes.

"Your art is remarkable," Willow said, her gaze on the painting before her. "It's as if I'm looking at a photograph."

Socks smiled, pride swelling within him at her praise. "Thank you," he said. "I strive to capture reality in my *creations."*

"Alright... Do you mind getting up for

a second?" she asked.

Socks found the question odd. "Why?" he asked.

"I... uh... would like to take a picture," Willow said.

Socks complied, getting up. Willow whipped a smartwatch out.

Willow positioned herself for a better view, and before he could react, a cascade of orange substance enveloped him, binding him in its sticky form. Panic surged through Socks as he struggled against the adhesive, his attempts to free himself met with frustration as he found himself immobilized.

"What's the meaning of this?" he snarled, straining to lift a paw, ready to charge.

It didn't budge. He tried again. He freed his foot, but it got stuck the moment it touched the grass again. Socks growled, before attempting to free himself by biting it. A curious crowd surrounded him.

Most of the crowd wore pure glee on their faces as Socks had earned their ire. Also, it wasn't every day one could treat a higher-ranking demon like that and not end up in a dungeon. But Socks hadn't hurt their feelings on purpose... It had been several instances of thoughtless comments. He wondered if Roxie and Brass were there, staring, eyeing him with pity. His friends would help if they were, right?

Socks's thoughts turned to his friends, their absence a glaring void in his time of need. Fear and uncertainty gnawed at his resolve and he pleaded for answers, desperate for reassurance that he wasn't alone in his suffering.

Maybe Socks had misjudged their friendship, and they were glad he was being humbled. He brushed the thought away. They were genuine friends. They wouldn't wish ill on him. But, if they were, why weren't they helping? He scanned the crowd. No sign of them.

The crowd jeered and taunted him, as most of the demons laughed. Socks closed his eyes. Maybe, if he pretended *he wasn't there, his magic wouldn't short circuit.*

"Now. How about I give you a new haircut?" the envy demon asked.

The audience gasped.

"You wouldn't dare," Socks growled, opening his eyes again.

"Yes, yes I would," she said, then took a few steps forward. She plucked one of his crest feathers.

Socks winced, then looked at the colorful feather in Willow's paw.

Willow tore his feathers out one by one, and Socks grappled with an isolation that cut deeper than any physical pain. He begged her to stop, but there was no use. He clung to the hope that his friends would come to his aid, their loyalty a beacon of light in the darkness that threatened to consume him. But they didn't, and nobody else intervened, allowing Willow to pluck him bald.

Socks slumped and huffed, leaving zel feeling helpless. Unsure of how to comfort him, and afraid to make him feel even worse, she consulted her smart lenses, searching for advice on how to console a traumatized familiar.

As lines of text appeared in her view, Zel read through them, hoping to find guidance and prevent an awkward silence.

"I'm sorry that happened to you. You didn't deserve it," she offered, her voice filled with genuine empathy, despite the robotic sentence structure. Continuing to read from the digital advice, she added, "Thank you for trusting me enough to share it."

Though Socks remained silent, Zel noticed his unease in his flicking tongue and shifting.

"I've heard experiences like that can leave a foul taste in your mouth. Just a moment," Zel said, excusing herself as she retreated indoors. Returning shortly after, she held a small plate of flan in one hand and a gleaming spoon in the other.

"Try this," Zel offered, placing the grocery store flan in front of Socks. She set the spoon on top before settling back onto the AeroCar.

Socks gave the dessert a curious sniff. It probably had cost the same as, if not more than, a whole box of flavorless, sugarless candy sold to cheer up Socks and his kind. Zel hadn't been lying when she said she knew nothing about pride demons.

He took a bite, and his eyes brightened with delight.

"It's so sweet, like essence. Tastes like yours, too," he said, his tail wagging. Zel let the comment slide and hoped he didn't figure that out the obvious way.

"Feeling any better?" Zel asked with a small smile.

"Yes, thanks," Socks said, surprising Zel with a big smile. It made her realize she may have judged pride demons from the one-sided anecdotes on the Internet and her one bad experience.

"The vets freed me by mixing oils and petroleum jelly and smearing it all over my fur. I ran off to the first hiding spot I could find. It was a cleaner room. There, I found Roxie and Brass tied up together. They gave me the most pitiful look ever. After I untied them, Roxie became blinded by rage and the cleaner's storage went up in hellfire. I hid in my dorm for days after. I didn't dare leave. My friends convinced me to go to the fighting pits one night with them to get out all my frustrations and to get a needed confidence boost," Socks said, looking down. He licked his chops again, and when that didn't work, he took another mouthful of flan.

"I'd hear others near my dorm door whispering things like 'It serves him right,' or 'Do you think he's ever coming out?' They'd taunt me, saying hurtful things, confident I wouldn't confront them. The day we met was the first day I'd left the dorm in a long time. I'm still unsure what her goal was," Socks explained.

Then his expression changed. He curled his lips into a snarl. "Which is why I want her to pay. I want revenge. I was very close to getting on with my plan, but then you arrived... But hey, now you understand, you'll buy me the clippers, right?" he asked.

Zel held in her laughter and had no clue what to say. She followed her heart. "I understand why you want revenge. There's no need to forgive her, you know? It would be unfair to yourself to do so," Zel said.

She shifted. Zel didn't know what to think about Willow anymore. She was obviously cruel... Like envy demons are said to be to be. Zel felt betrayed, yet numb. Everyone made mistakes, and people could change, but she didn't want to attune to Willow anymore. As the silence took over, Zel's emotions urged her to say something.

Following her heart was a terrible idea. Would she say something impulsive and hurt his feelings, like she'd done all along? She thought it over and over, then decided it would be better to say it. "But do you really want to make her suffer as much as you did?" Zel asked.

"Yes. I already chose a less cruel way of doing it. Isn't that enough?" Socks asked.

She hoped he would reconsider. Zel was about to say something when her smartwatch rang again. It was her mom. She denied the call. She still needed more time.

"Hey, Zel," Vih called. She, Koa and Star carried several bags filled with candles as they came closer.

"I found the perfect place for us to set up the ritual," Vih said.

"Great. While you do that, I'll go back to the store with Koa," Socks said, earning an odd look from everyone.

"Why?" Koa asked.

"Vih needs to set up the ritual, and it would be best if Zel was with her... I want to buy something and don't want to do so alone," Socks said.

Zel was sure by something, he meant clippers and had realized she wouldn't let him.

"But we need a demon to light the candles. Magic has an odd lighting order, and I'm pretty sure it comes naturally to demons, but it's hard for us humans," Vih said.

"Star may not look it, but I'm sure he's a demon too," Socks said, receiving a look from Star.

Koa sighed. "It is fine. I can take him shopping, then check on that Heart Stone to see if there is anything I can do."

And just like that, it was settled. Zel, Star, and Vih went one way, and Koa and Socks the other.

CHAPTER 23

Zel stood by Vih in the most secluded parking lot they could find, one near some trees. Vih drew a circle with a bunch of intelligible letters on it with a white chalk and placed a bunch of colorful birthday candles all around it, as Star lit each electric wick with care.

"I wonder, does magic count this as one or two candles?" Vih asked, looking at a two-wicked candle shaped like a cake slice.

"Erm... are you sure these will be fine? I haven't heard of demons using birthday candles in their rituals before. Isn't magic strict?" Zel asked, trying to hide her unease.

"The thing about magic is it's too vague. Science moves forward by figuring out how things work, but magic? It advances when we figure out how things don't work. Ever notice how spells are never that specific? It's always 'eye of newt,' never 'eye of swordtail newt.' That's because the ingredients aren't as important as you'd think. A lot of it's symbolic or 'close enough.' There was this demon influencer who showed us how to do a spell that needed an eye of newt, but they made it work with a glass eye from a newt plushie. But yeah, ingredients do matter... just a little. Like, I tried summoning a familiar and ended up with a plant monster. Whoops. I thought I could make a few swaps. But hey, these birthday candles I used instead of the creepy red ones? Totally shouldn't affect the ritual."

Zel couldn't shake the feeling that they teetered on the edge of disaster. She kept quiet, and watched Vih place the goofy candles.

"Hey Zel, you're not still mad at me, are you? I mean, there are a few things I'm still holding onto, like you breaking my laptop and knocking out my molar without so much as an

147

apology. I was kind of hoping you'd mention that when you showed up at my door, or even later at Burger&Burger, or maybe after meeting Hawke. But you acted like nothing happened."

Vih's frustration simmered, a weight she'd carried since the start of their journey.

Vih's words settled upon Zel, and she was unsure of how to react. "Look, Vih, I'm sorry. I may have overreacted a bit, and I should have found a better way to handle things," she said genuinely. Zel did feel sorry. She knew she was wrong and should have done something about it.

Vih paused her drawing to regard Zel, her expression expectant. "I'm not ready to forgive you yet, though. Not until we talk about why we were fighting in the first place. I still don't understand what set you off."

Zel's frustration bubbled to the surface once more. "Because you cheated on the test! You took my notes, reviewed them before the exam, and left me helpless! Then you didn't even return my tablet, and I had to pay the school's ridiculous fine for a new one!" Zel's voice changed tone, but that simmering, explosive anger of the past was gone.

"What? No, I didn't!" Vih's denial was swift, her shock almost convincing.

"Yes, you did. My tablet was in your drawer. I saw it there, connected the dots, got angry, and punched you in the face. That wasn't the best course of action, obviously, but you can't deny it's mine. It has the same anemone cover!" Zel said.

"No! I would never! That was my tablet! I saw a cover like yours and bought it so we could match. I even sent you messages before buying it," Vih said, then pulled her tablet out of her pocket.

Zel took it and eyed it. The cover was the same, but the tablet was pink, while Zel's was turquoise. She tried unlocking the screen, only to see Vih's name show up under "Welcome." Then she returned the device and checked her smartwatch for messages. Vih was blocked, but she checked the last chat. There were several photos of a tablet covering just like hers, then a message:

Look at what I found! Our tablets will be twinsies now; can't wait to show it to you.

Zel didn't know what to say.

Maybe Vih had this convoluted lie planned from the start... To steal my notes and keep my friendship... What am I thinking? That's ridiculous. I need to stop being so... anxious... Okay, some of it is important, but is it worth worrying about everything all the time? No. I'll try to stop.

"If you still don't believe me, you can check your note edit history. You'll see that no one accessed the documents," Vih said.

"I believe you. I'm sorry too. I overreacted. I jumped to conclusions," Zel said. *Just as I did with Socks's kind. I gave you no opening, or for pride demons to explain their intentions. I just assumed what they were, never letting them explain themselves. It won't hurt to look past first impressions. Things are never as shallow as I think they are.*

"I should've asked you about it, then freaked out. I'm sorry I broke your tooth... It must have been expensive to fix..." she said, a little shy. "I'll try to be more reasonable next time..." Zel said.

"I understand. I'm unsure if I forgive you. It was expensive to fix, the laptop was too," Vih said.

If Zel and Vih were younger, they would have sworn to never fight like that again. But they were sixteen. They knew things could get turbulent. Saying they'd never fight again would be a lie. But with hope, they could go back to being as close as they once were.

"Done, dears. All candles lit," Star said, his arrival providing a moment of levity, drawing them back to the present. Zel stared at the ring of candles and couldn't help but feel hopeful for the future, knowing their bond had resisted the misunderstanding.

"Okay, all set. Now we just need Socks and Koa," Vih announced, wiping the sweat from her forehead.

"We're here," Koa announced. Socks held a small package.

"Is it all settled?" the pride demon asked.

"Should be. Now we just need to get you and Zel ready," Vih said.

Zel's smartwatch rang again. It was her mom. She answered. Zel felt it had been long enough and that they should make up... In fact, she even forgot she had meant to be mad.

CHAPTER 24

Zel answered the call, and a hologram projected in front of her.

"Hi, Mom," Zel said, thinking up an apology.

"Haha, hello," the figure replied.

That's not Mom, Zel realized, and her breath caught when she saw Chili. The razorback's goggles made her even scarier, especially since she was in Zel's apartment.

"I was starting to wonder what teenager ignores multiple calls from her mom," Chili said, then panned the camera to Zel's mom and Luma, both tied up to a chair. Luma had a muzzle on, and silver tape covered Mom's mouth. They were in the center of a comically large bear trap-like device.

"Mom! Luma!" Zel cried out. That couldn't be happening.

"You have two hours to bring me your familiar, or else..." Chili said, then panned to a smaller version of the contraption. She placed a twig that looked like a person in the middle. The moment she removed her paw, the trap snapped shut, arrows hit the twig, it caught fire, then two massive logs crashed into it, also catching fire.

Zel stared, open-mouthed.

"That's a bit... excessive," Vih said.

Chili filmed herself again. "I'm waiting. And don't even try calling law enforcement. What I'm doing is completely legal!" she said, then hung up.

Zel stood there in shock. Koa cursed. The vet student was in a heated phone call. They hung up and rolled their eyes.

"Can you believe that? The law enforcement dispatcher bot told me razorbacks can use any method they see fit, and it's not their place to help us!" they grumbled.

Socks paced, trying to decide what to do. Shades of

blue and purple painted the sky, and the air filled with rustling leaves and distant city sounds. He stood at the edge of the sigil, staring at passersby, but not really seeing them.

Zel approached.

"Socks?" she said. No answer. She sat beside him and placed a hand on his back.

He looked at her, startled. "Oh... I didn't see you. I was... distracted," he said.

"What's on your mind?" she asked, her voice gentle but concerned.

He turned to her with sorrowful eyes. "Zel, I... I need to do something on my own."

Zel jumped to her feet. "Now? You need to do something on your own now, even though my family is being held hostage because of you?"

Socks closed his eyes. "Yes. That's why I need to go."

"No! You are solving this mess! You aren't going anywhere until my mom and Luma are safe! We need to stick together to save them!"

Socks shook his head. "I have a plan, but you won't approve, so I'm not telling you."

"No!" Zel shouted. Vih, Koa, and Star, who had been discussing their next steps, turned their attention to the conversation. Vih stepped forward, concerned.

"Socks, we'll figure something out! You can't just run off!" Zel said.

"This conversation is a waste of time! Time we don't have. I've made up my mind, bye!" Socks said, then darted through the parking lot.

"Wait!" Zel yelled and ran after him.

She ran for a long time, but Socks was faster. He ran under AeroCars to lose her, and eventually, it worked. Zel had no idea where Socks had gone. She only saw stores, crowds, and parked vehicles as she panted.

"Socks!" she yelled. There was no answer. Zel cried. "You are a selfish coward; do you hear me? You are a coward!" she sobbed.

Vih caught up then and led her back to the candle circle. "We will think of a plan. I'm sure we will," Vih said.

CHAPTER 25

Back at the candle circle, Zel paced, her eyes darting to the smartwatch's clock every few seconds. Each tick amplified her anxiety. The alley's tall walls made it feel like it was closing in on her.

"Socks ran off! I can't believe he's just... Disappeared! Is he that selfish? I..." Zel started, glancing at the candles and pacing more.

"We need a plan, and fast... Here's a plan of my flat. Zel's is the same," Vih said, projecting a hologram of the floor plan. "We can't just rush in there without knowing what we're up against."

"There must be a way to break in without getting caught... What about the window?" Koa asked, rifling through the hologram.

"The window is on the seventieth floor. We'd need to fly there," Vih said.

"How about we take the AeroCar and crash it through the window? Yes, that's it. Let's do it!" Zel said, trembling.

"Uh... that will cause more harm than good," Vih said.

Zel stopped pacing and leaned over the hologram. She pinched it to zoom out to see the whole corridor, her fingers tracing the intricate pathways. "Even if we get in, how do we free my family? And what if they've already moved her?" Her voice cracked, betraying her fear.

Star, who had been quietly observing, placed a comforting paw on Zel's shoe. "We'll rescue her, dear. We just need to stay focused. Panicking won't help"

"Star! Can't you turn into a raven? Fly up there? You're a kindness angel, right? Shouldn't you be a raven already?"

"That's not how that works, I'm afraid... But even if it was, I'd fly up there... and what? Peck the window?"

"We could give you glass cutters! Or wait outside the door and..." Zel facepalmed. It wasn't a good plan.

Zel took a deep breath, steadying herself. She turned to Vih. "What do we know about their defenses? How can we disable them?"

Vih tapped on the hologram, a room at the end of the corridor. "This section here is where their power source is. If we can disrupt it, we might cause a blackout. It won't last long, backup generators and all, but it might be enough to get in and out."

"Terrible idea! We're facing a covet demon and pride demon. They can see in the dark, we'd be the ones at a disadvantage!" Koa said.

"If the idea was to stun them by turning the lights back on at maximum brightness, their new fancy sunglasses ruin our plan," Star said.

Zel took a deep breath. Laughter startled her, and she looked across the parking lot at some children, pointing and looking at them. She wondered what they were laughing at. Probably at the gigantic magic sigil on the pavement.

"We could use a distraction," Star suggested. "Something big enough to draw their attention from us."

Zel nodded. "What kind of distraction?"

Star pondered. "No idea"

Zel looked at the clock again in frustration. She couldn't shake the feeling of time slipping away, that every second brought her mother closer to death. She looked at her friends, their faces set in confusion. They were risking everything for her, for her family. But they were all teens. They had no clue what to do. If there even was something to do.

"Thank you," she whispered, her voice filled with gratitude, and she wiped her eyes with a sleeve. "But this isn't working. Miraculous plans aren't the way to go. Time is passing. We've been planning for over forty minutes. So much wasted time! I'll head over to reason with them. At least explain that Socks is missing and beg them to not hurt my family."

"Talking it out is such a you thing to do," Koa muttered, and they didn't mean it in a good way. Star headbutted them in the shin to shut them up.

The vet hopped on a single foot in anger. "What? Am I lying?" they growled.

The others exchanged sad looks.

Vih gave her a reassuring smile. "We're in this together, Zel. I'll go with you,"

Star placed a paw on each of her feet and looked up at her. "And we'll make sure my dear Socks is safe, too."

Zel's heart clenched at the mention of Socks. She couldn't bear the thought of him, not after he'd run off in selfishness. She pushed the fear aside. The razorbacks weren't mercenaries, murderers, or things like that. They were... extreme border patrol. That meant they could be reasoned with, right?

Zel hurried to the AeroCar to make it home in time. The others followed her.

CHAPTER 26

Zel reached her apartment hallway with time to spare, but she still ran as fast as she could. Koa, Vih, and Star rushed behind her. Zel threw her door open.

"Let my mom go! Please! Socks ran off. I don't know where he is. We can agree on something, but plea—" Zel stopped when she saw her mom and Luma standing there, unbound and safe, in the middle of an argument.

"Mom!" Zel cried, then hugged her mom for a long time.

"Zel! I'm glad you're okay!"

"I'm glad you're fine too, Mom," she said, then picked up Luma. "And you, Luma, I am so sorry!" Tears welled in Zel's eyes.

"I'm glad you're okay," the schnauzer said, wagging her tail as Zel put her down again.

Zel looked around the flat. It was messier than usual, but held no death traps or razorbacks.

"What happened? Why did they let you go? I need to find Socks, to tell him you're fine, then give him a stern talking to about selfishness and—" She stopped when she saw her mom and Luma's sad gazes.

"I'm afraid you won't see him again," Luma said.

"What? Why?" Zel asked, anger rising. She'd find him.

"Zel, listen. A few moments ago..."

Her mom and Luma had been tied up while razorbacks paced the room.

"Hey, spicy stew!" Socks called from the doorway.

Chili glared at him. "It's Chili, as in chili pepper, not as in... Ugh."

"I give myself up. I surrender. Release Zel's family," Socks said.

"Is that so?" Chili asked, pleased. She approached, pinned Socks down, and pressed on his neck to make him spit out the soul. She grabbed the shiny, levitating orb with care.

"His magic is too unstable to unattune. Let's have a doctor check him out," Chili said to her colleagues, who then lunged at Socks. Castan placed a muzzle on Socks as Spark tied his front paws behind his back.

"Remember to restrain him well. We don't want his pride demon natural weapons being a nuisance," Chili said, watching.

Then she turned to Zel's mom. She snapped her fingers, and the bear-trap around the humans disappeared in a bright red light, like embers. Chili approached Zel's mom and reached out a paw. Mom closed her eyes, bracing for the pain of the tape being removed, but Chili snapped her fingers again, and the ropes and tape disappeared in embers. Mom looked to her side and saw a freed Luma pawing her snout.

Chili joined her colleagues, who held Socks and waited in front of a bright square portal shimmering with energy displaying the distorted landscape of Hell. The razorbacks jumped through, and it closed. Then it reopened, and Chili threw Zel's soul back into the human world. The portal closed again. The soul dashed for the window, trying to reunite with its physical form.

"What?" Zel repeated, looking into her mom's eyes. "So, is Socks... gone? Did he... No! I told him we'd figure something out! Why did he... No!" Zel shouted, then hugged her mom again.

Part of her was glad Socks had sacrificed himself, but she was also angry she'd never see him again.

"I told him we'd find a way. We would've found a way to save you both," Zel said.

Her mom tried to soothe her with a tighter hug. Vih, Koa, and Star loitered by the door.

Her smartwatch rang. She looked at the notification. It was from the Maritime Expedition. She opened it. It read:

Dear Zel, your Maritime Expedition application won't progress further. Do not reply to this message or contact us about this.

Zel's world fell apart. The news hit her like an F5 tornado, uprooting large trees and destroying everything in its path. She forgot about Socks, the razorbacks, and the dangers her mom had been in. The whole adventure vanished from her mind.

"They can't have made their decision already! It's too early! I studied so hard! I aced every exam! I..." Tears streamed down her face. Zell trembled. The email said not to call them, but she did and yelled at the robot who answered. She demanded to know why they denied her a chance to matter, but it just repeated that she shouldn't call and hung up.

Zel groaned and tried again, only to get the notification that they had blocked her number. She screamed, then rushed over to her mom.

"Give me your smartwatch! I'm calling them again!" she demanded.

Her mom moved back. "No, no, you aren't. It's fine," Mom said, trying to keep Zel from reaching her wrist.

"I need to know why I failed! Maybe it was a mistake! Let me call again!" She raised her voice as tears ran down her cheeks.

"Zel, you're so talented. There will be more chances. This just wasn't meant to be."

"I don't want more chances! I wanted this one! I don't want to hear about fate! People who say that don't care! It's a cheap, lazy phrase people use when they can't be bothered to help!"

"It is just one rejection. There are so many other places to study and..."

"Stop giving me empty words and hand the smartwatch over! Listen to me for once! Pretend you understand how much this matters to me!" Zel jumped at her mom, who held her back.

"Lashing out at me won't change anything! Everyone gets rejected! Life is more than chasing pointless dreams! Stop acting like a child! Are you five, throwing a tantrum like this? Aren't you embarrassed to subject your friends to this?" Mom said.

Zel stopped. Then, she noticed Luma biting her sock, trying to pull her away, and Vih, Koa, and Star were still by the door, pretending not to pay attention. Vih looked at the nearest wall. Koa checked their smartwatch and Star covered his eyes. The humans' cheeks had flushed, despite their fake disinterest in the situation.

Zel wiped at her face.

"There will be other opportunities, ones you can't see yet. And you'll be ready for them because of everything you've done so far," Luma said, letting go of the sock.

"Please, I need to be alone for a moment," Zel said, heading for the flat's bathroom, the only place with privacy. She closed the door carefully and sat under the sink. The razorbacks had gotten what they wanted, so they weren't in danger anymore.

"It's all my fault... My mom and Luma almost got hurt, and Socks will burn in a volcano..." she muttered. If she hadn't gone to the rescue center, none of that would have happened.

CHAPTER 27

In Hell, Socks trudged through a red cave, dragged by his arms by Chili and Spark as Castan took the lead. The air was thick with sulfur and the heat so intense it nearly scorched his skin. Magic lights cast eerie glows, and towering stalagmites merged into the ceiling, forming natural pillars. Lava glowed from cracks in the walls, adding to the oppressive atmosphere.

Despite the discomfort, Socks found some comfort in the rocky landscape and stifling heat. He had missed it.

"I can't believe you went through all the trouble of running around just to make a heroic, brainless sacrifice. Are you expecting a medal? Maybe you thought we'd let you go because of your selflessness?" Castan mocked.

Socks stayed silent. He'd acted because it was unfair for someone else to suffer for his mistakes, and because Zel would've lost her family if he hadn't intervened. He knew he was at fault. If he'd been more compassionate, like Zel wanted, he wouldn't have fallen off the roof in the first place.

They walked under empty cages hanging from the ceiling until Castan halted. Chili and Spark stopped too, exchanging puzzled looks.

"Is everything alright?" Spark asked.

"I sense silver. Are you sure we're going the right way?" Castan asked, uneasy.

"This place is called the Silverworks for a reason. Now come on, keep walking," Chili said. Socks noticed Castan's discomfort. He should've been used to silver magic.

Light illuminated a section of the corridor ahead, revealing a window displaying a demon tied down. Two constructs held him as a soldier in gleaming silver armor heated a branding iron in a lava pool. Socks watched, memories of his time as a silversmith flooding back.

"What did he do?" Castan asked, stopping to peer into the room.

"Who? The demon tied up?" Chili asked.

"Yes. Someone wants to brand him with silver of all things. He must have done something serious," Castan said.

Socks found Castan's ignorance odd. Chili and Spark exchanged concerned glances. Castan had worked there and used to oversee the Silverworks.

"The demon is there willingly. We tie them up to prevent squirming and ruining the brand. The silver brand allows for permanent residency in the human world. It may seem cruel, but no one can fake it and it ensures they always have their documentation," Spark explained.

"You say it can't be faked, but how did our prisoner fake it, then?" Castan asked, lifting Socks's hand to inspect the scar.

Chili examined his palm. "That isn't fake. Silver caused the scar, but it isn't as deep as it should be. It's a little skewed. The Silversmith did a rather poor job on this one," she said, staring at Socks.

"Excuse me, I want to check it." Chili ran her thumb over the scar. "I thought you'd be branded with iron or a silver alloy, which is the most common form of forgery. But your visa has the seal of the Silverworks, and all the documentation is listed... Hmm... It says that you had the visa approved by... Silversmith Lataleumaeus?" she asked, shocked.

"Hey, Spark, what's our prisoner's name and profession again?" Chili asked. Spark checked a magical tablet.

"Lataleumaeus, a Silversmith," she read, then looked at Socks. They all stared at him.

"So you thought you could fake the documents and approve yourself without anyone finding out?" Castan sneered.

"You know very well that's not what happened! Every

164

document is authentic! The only iffy part was the brand! Besides, why are you talking like this? If the truth comes out, you'll get the worst punishment, not me!" Socks snapped. Spark tugged on the chain to shush him.

"Don't tell lies like that. Such insolence won't be tolerated," Castan threatened.

"If anyone is lying here, it's you! When I couldn't get other silversmiths to approve it, you said I could do it myself, that it wasn't illegal. The problem was, I couldn't physically brand myself because I had to be tied up. After some failed attempts with a pretend branding rod, you offered to do it! That's what makes my brand not authentic. I remember you freaked out and held back a bit, which is why the scar isn't as deep as it should be and is a little crooked. So, if I get executed for having an inauthentic brand, you should too, for forgery!" Socks growled.

Castan punched him in the face. Socks staggered, but Spark held him up, and prevented him from falling.

"That's ridiculous and never happened," Castan said.

They continued, passing torture racks, hovering constructs, and other Silverworks employees, until they reached the dungeon. The cells were etched into the rocky walls, housing prisoners caught smuggling, crossing realms illegally, or being extradited.

Spark opened a cell, and Chili motioned to Castan. He steered Socks into the cell, and Chili swept his hind legs with her tail and pushed him in, locking the cell with both Socks and Castan inside. Socks was surprised.

"What! Chili, let me out! What are you doing?" Castan shouted, gripping the bars.

"Your friend here said some... potentially worrisome things," Chili said.

"It isn't true!"

Chili and Spark exchanged looks. She didn't explain

further. She just left. Spark gave them both an empathetic look before walking away, and Castan yelled they were making a mistake and that something was wrong.

"Great! Are you happy you locked me here with you?" Castan asked.

Socks, meanwhile, leaned against the wall, wondering how Zel was, if her mom was alright. He reflected on his life. It had been good, with a few regrets, but who didn't have those? If they threw him in a volcano at such a young age, at least he could say he had a nice life.

Castan, who still fumed, interrupted his thoughts. "This is a mistake! They don't know what they're doing."

Eventually, Castan gave up and leaned against the opposing wall.

Socks studied Castan. "So... how's things been?"

Castan's eyes widened, then narrowed. "What does it matter? You're as good as dead." he sighed. "And so am I, apparently."

"It doesn't. But hey, next time, try not to act like a total jerk to your best friend."

Castan had totally forgotten Socks and himself were best friends. Maybe it wasn't the best situation... But could he complete his mission by being a tad more... amicable? He told a couple of life stories based on his research, then he invented a couple of things, and planned to ask Socks about how he got into this mess when he finished.

CHAPTER 28

Zel sat on the bathroom floor, her head resting on her knees as she sat beneath the sink. The cold tiles pressed against her skin, grounding her in the overwhelming sense of loss and meaninglessness. She felt trapped in a void, her thoughts swirling in a dark haze.

A knock sounded at the door. "It's me," Vih said.

"And me," Koa added.

"Come in," Zel said. She hadn't locked the door. As they entered, Star trailed behind them, holding a familiar treat shaped like a bone.

"I brought something sweet to cheer you up," Star said, handing Zel the treat. "You might like it. Koa always dives for the treat jar when I'm not looking."

Zel managed a small smile, and she looked at Koa, whose face flushed a deep red. She took a bite. It tasted like chocolate, with a hint of something else, something comforting.

"Thanks, Star. You're very kind," Zel said, giving him a gentle pat.

Vih sat beside Zel. "I was looking through some old pictures. Do you remember this day?" Vih asked, projecting a hologram from her smartwatch of a younger version of Vih and Zel on an aquarium school field trip. They barely knew each other then, paired together because neither had friends nor wanted to be alone in the pictures. The holograms showed them in front of penguins, squids, seahorses, surrounded by jellyfish in a tunnel, and many other scenes.

"I remember you wouldn't stop talking about the animals. You knew more than our guide," Zel said, a small smile forming. "We broke off and explored on our own, then the teacher found us, and we got in trouble. You awakened my love for sea creatures..." Zel's smile faded. "Learning about

167

them used to be fun. But I can't remember the last time studying the sea felt like anything other than a chore I have to do to be someone."

She wiped her tears. The hologram shifted to a video of her and Vih goofing around, dressed up as astronauts, vets, doctors, and explorers. They made plans for a hopeful future full of possibilities—possibilities that were still there.

Just because one out of many marine biology programs rejected her didn't mean there wouldn't be others. "I don't need to study at Madlen University to matter or to be someone," she realized. "Everyone who studies there is someone, but people who study elsewhere are someone too." She felt much lighter realizing that.

"I know several places that teach sea life," Koa said. "Some are looking for volunteers. I can send you their names."

"I don't have a familiar, so I can't fully relate. But if you're willing to take a risk, I think I know a way to bring Socks back," Vih said, her voice steady but filled with hope.

Zel gazed into Vih's eyes.

"False hope is hurtful," Koa interjected.

"It's not false," Vih insisted. "Listen, we could get him back here legally. If he's still alive. The hard part would be keeping him here. Not because the razorbacks would chase him, but because he'd have to return once he completed his task. We need to find a nearly impossible task."

Zel's brow furrowed, trying to follow Vih's plan.

"Oh no, no! No one knows how to do that anymore," Koa protested.

"How to do what?" Zel asked, her frustration bubbling.

"I do. Remember Zel? You saw me summon a plant from their dimension! Okay, it wasn't my best attempt, but still... Socks is a demon. All we need to do is summon him the old-fashioned way," Vih said, a grin spreading across her face.

Zel's eyes widened, a spark of hope igniting within

her. "You can really do that?"

Vih nodded. "Yes! Well... maybe. Probably. It's risky and we'll need to be careful, but it isn't a 'no, I can't.' We can try."

For the first time in what felt like an eternity, Zel felt a glimmer of light pierce the darkness. She wasn't alone. She had her friends, and together, they had a plan.

"Know what's the best part? We already have the summoning circle ready. We were just going to use it for an unattuning ritual instead," Vih said.

CHAPTER 29

Chili and Spark walked through the cavernous Silverworks corridors, their armor clanking with each step. Constructs hovered around them, their magic cores glowing, powering their swift, agitated movements. Demons hurried after the constructs, moving away from Chili and Spark.

"This doesn't make any sense! The shapeshifter is here for information, Spark, but I have no idea what he could possi—" Chili began, only to crash into a demon.

"What are you doing?" she demanded.

The demon looked at her with a calm, yet wary expression, typical of someone who had bumped into a higher-ranking demon and didn't want to escalate the situation. "Didn't you hear? A shapeshifter escaped his cell," the demon explained. Chili and Spark exchanged a look. Both had muted their magical tablets, as usual.

"The one I brought in? But we just came from the dungeon level. The constructs detected nothing! He can't just show up in the main hall undetected!" Chili exclaimed, frustration filling her voice. She stopped and raced after the crowd. She arrived at the main hall, skidding to a halt, to find demons and constructs restraining and adding metal bands to the wings of an orange pride demon. Chili would recognize that face anywhere. It was Castan.

"How did he get out?" she asked.

"Apparently, he just walked in and triggered the constructs' signals," Spark said. Chili found it odd. Why not flee to freedom? Soon, she and Spark escorted Castan back to the lower levels. He attempted to talk, but Chili told him to shut it or else. He obeyed, though clearly annoyed.

CHAPTER 19

CHAPTER 30

"It's good to catch up," Socks said, concluding his tale of how he ended up with Zel. But Castan's expression remained... grumpy, lacking the expected amusement.

A construct flew past their cell bars.

"Yes, it is nice. Say, back at our place, you often brought in human world magazines and items... Where did you get all that?"

Castan's question sent a shiver down Socks's spine, a pang of embarrassment washing over him. How did Castan know about that? Did he see Socks sneaking in late at night or during work hours?

"Oh, they were... uh... work-related," Socks stumbled over his words, attempting to defend himself. Castan's skepticism was clear. "Right, Castan, look. They were apprehended items..." Socks began, attempting to salvage the situation.

"That many?" Castan's inquiry cut through Socks's explanation, leaving him sighing in defeat.

"At least it's what I always said they were when I turned them in. I logged each one for investigation and may have spent a bit of work time perusing them instead of focusing on my tasks. It's not uncommon for demons who cross portals to bring items with them. I suppose I raised a few eyebrows with the sheer quantity of magazines I had, but most chalked it up to my job at the Silverworks," Socks confessed, hoping Castan would understand.

"That's quite cunning of you. What happened to them?" Castan asked, his tone implying a mixture of admiration and condescension that left Socks feeling uneasy.

"Uh, thanks," Socks muttered, unsure of how to

respond to it. "As for the magazines, they've been destroyed. It's department policy...And I feared someone would find out if I kept them."

"Wait, every single one?" Castan's terror caught Socks off guard.

"Uh... No. I saved my favorite ones. I even brought some over with me to the human plane," Socks said, watching Castan's demeanor shift.

"Did you ever notice something odd on the pages? Especially on the ones you saved? Could I look at them? Look. A friend is looking for something. Something we really need to find. Demons will starve to death if we don't. Some writing in the dialect of the angels. A recipe, measurements, techniques, or anything of the sort?" Castan asked.

Does this have anything to do with the recipe Harper is looking for? Socks thought. *I will lie, just in case... I don't want Harper finding that out.*

"No," Socks said, though he remembered one that fit that description.

"Maybe some loose sheets, or something you couldn't make sense of?"

"No. May I know... why the fuss over this one recipe?" Socks asked.

"It's Dryas's... uh... imitation of soul essence. He created a pretty close copy. We need it back soon. Do you understand? Things are going bad in Hell, very bad, and it will only get worse if we don't get that back!" Castan said.

Chili and Spark, stopping in front of them, interrupted their conversation.

Socks leaned against the wall. He glanced at them, then looked to his side, surprised to see Castan there, leaning on the opposite wall. The Castan they held looked equally surprised. Either they had locked up the real one, or they were about to lock him up. There was only one way to figure it out.

Chili clapped her hands three times, and her magic tablet lit up. "Get me a magic mirror," she commanded.

Moments later, a construct flew in, holding a handheld mirror in one of its arms. It handed the mirror to Chili. She checked her reflection. It was her, as it should be. Then she pointed it at the Castan by her side. It reflected him. Finally, she pointed it at the Castan in the cell. The mirrored image changed, revealing a generosity angel with white feathers instead of hair and a yellow halo—a shapeshifter.

"Malah..." she cursed. "Well, Castan, we have catching up to do."

"You FRAUD!" Socks growled, then threw himself on top of the shapeshifter, starting a fight despite his restraints.

Chili and Spark tried to get them to stop, and several constructs flew over to help.

Soon Socks was thrown in a new cell, while the shapeshifter, with a black eye, a bloody nose, and several other scrapes, stayed in the previous one, shooting Socks a death glare.

Chili, Spark and true Castan, headed to a staffroom of the silverworks, and Castan's voice cut through the corridor: "You went on a mission without backup?"

Several demons slowed their steps, ears pricked with interest.

Chili and Spark sat in the cushioned chairs, their expressions tense as Castan paced, his tail lashing with frustration.

"That's reckless! You can't go out without me or another demon in my role. You've put me in a bind, again."

"Can you sit down for a second?" Chili asked, her tone firm. "I haven't even explained yet. All I said was that we went on a mission—"

"Alone. You went alone," he repeated, shaking his head. "Do you know how many times this has happened

175

because I trusted you to lead? This isn't some game, Chili."

Chili bit her lip, the guilt creeping in. "About... five or six times?"

"Seven. This makes it ten!" Castan's frustration burned through his voice.

"Wait, that can't be right..." Spark muttered, frowning as she tried to check the math mentally.

Chili shifted in her seat, the weight of Castan's disappointment pressing down on her. She never meant for things to go wrong, or to drag her friends into messes.

Spark jumped in, her voice calmer. "We took the shapeshifter with us when we went on the mission. We thought he was, well, you."

Castan stopped mid-step, finally registering the detail. "You didn't? Well, that's something... but still, you couldn't tell it wasn't me?"

Chili leaned back, flashing a half-smile. "Oh, I knew. You were being a jerk, more than usual."

Castan shot her a glare. "If anyone's a jerk here, it's you." He sighed heavily. "Now, why is my best friend sitting in a cell?"

"The Silversmith? For fraud. In fact, you should be too, according to him," Chili explained.

Castan stopped pacing.

"Fraud? How so?"

Chili explained the most unprofessional mission she had ever done in her lifetime.

CHAPTER 31

Zel, Koa, and Star stood around the candle circle in the parking lot. The electronic candles flickered eerily in the daylight as Vih redrew the markings on the ground.

"Wait, Vih, you're making a mistake. You forgot the In'lu sigils. Without them, we'll summon the demon instantly. It could be in the middle of something!" Star explained.

Vih didn't look up. "I did it on purpose. Socks is probably in a dungeon or tied to a torture rack. An instant summon might be the best thing for him.

"But before we proceed, a warning," Vih continued, standing up. "Demons have powerful instincts. Socks might get 'soul crazed' and try to eat your essence. It's rare, but if it happens, it can be traumatic."

The warning sent a shiver down Zel's spine. "Soul-crazed," she repeated, the term chilling her. She had heard about demons who lost touch with reason and had instinct overtake them. They often sought souls. Some returned to themselves after gathering enough, others needed an incentive to stop their rampage ... Incentives such as a tranquilizer dart.

"I understand, but I want to bring him back," Zel said, her voice steady, though her hands trembled.

"Alright. Zel, bring the offering," Vih instructed.

Zel set down a bowl of blue, glowing bone-shaped familiar treats.

"We are skipping the sacrifice," Vih said.

"I thought sacrifices were a fresh soul to prevent the demon from taking the summoner's," Koa said.

"It will work without one," Vih assured them.

"I'm more worried about the summoner's soul than with decorum," Koa muttered.

Vih didn't respond, adding to Zel's unease. "The

important thing is to bring Socks back, right?" Vih asked.

Zel got a brief feeling Vih was hiding something.

"Now for the material offering! Bring the dough!" Vih declared.

Zel placed a five-dollar Trashmart gift card near the circle, which also glowed blue.

Star facepalmed. "This is painful to watch. I never understood how humans could mess up simple magic, but now I get it..."

"Now, we need Socks's demon name. Do you know it?"

Zel remembered the war scene. "It's Lataleumaeus."

Star looked puzzled. "That sounds like a typo. Are you sure it's not Atalaeumaeus?"

"I'm sure," Zel said.

Vih put on some music and handed Zel a tablet with a chant. As Zel and Star read it, the electric candle's "flames" flickered, and blue light spread across the drawing.

CHAPTER 32

Back in the Silverworks, Socks sat in his lonely cell, tapping his pointy tail on the stone floor when a Castan approached, imposing as always, wings folded into a pretty arch. He held a magic mirror up. It still reflected him. He was the true Castan.

"Hello, long time no see," Socks said.

"Long time indeed. Do you know what this is?" Castan unrolled a yellowed scroll.

Socks glanced at it. "A Haya letter?"

"Exactly. This one has your silversmith seal and higher-ranking demons' approval of the branding being done by me. It was never a fraud."

"I thought they had denied it and we did it anyway," Socks admitted.

Castan rolled his eyes.

So... Was all this running for nothing? Why did they even come after me?

"As if I'd do something like that," he said. "As for the shapeshifter, we've taken him to questioning. He's said some interesting things so far, but I think a more experienced torturer will get more info out of him."

"So, am I free to go?" Socks's tail thumped in excitement.

Castan's smile faded. "I'm afraid we still have to hold you. For smuggling."

"What? I've never smuggled anything!"

"The shapeshifter said you possessed human media that could cause freewill. Those are banned because any demon developing freewill here would be miserable. Now I see how you went from content to wanting to leave and become an architect in such a short time. Apparently, this

179

whole nonsense was to get those from you. A fake mission my colleagues got dragged into."

Socks thumped his tail in indignation.

Latalaeumaeus Socks heard.

"Tell whoever is calling my name I'm here," he grumbled.

Castan blinked. "No one is calling your name."

Lataleumaeus.

"There it is again! Someone is calling me! Get them here now!" Socks insisted, feeling an odd pull. He recognized the voice. Zel's voice.

"There's no one calling you," Castan said, worried.

"Yes! Someone is! Bring them here, or I'll go to them!" Socks demanded, struggling with his instincts. Socks threw himself at the cell bars, trying to break free, to find the one calling him. Castan jumped and called for help. Constructs and nearby demons rushed over.

Socks growled, thrashed, and scratched the walls with his wings. He needed to get out. He needed to find the source of the call. Thin constructs slid through the cell bars to check on Socks.

He wanted soul essence. He needed it.

Socks disappeared from the cell in a puff of magic. A split second after materializing in the human world, he took possession of the soul, bit it, and started draining it.

CHAPTER 33

Zel and the others stood by the summoning circle, then a tower of blue light emerged from it. It reached for the sky. Then Zel fainted. The only reason she didn't hit the ground was because Vih caught her.

"Zel! Lie her down. I'll hold her legs at a ninety-degree angle," Koa said.

"That won't work... It's not a lack of oxygen, but a lack of soul," Vih explained, gently laying Zel on the ground.

"What? What happened to hers?" Koa asked.

"Well... there was no sacrifice..." Vih said with a shy smile.

"What is that supposed to mean?" Koa said.

"It means my dear Socks has it. He disconnected it from her physical form," Star said, looking at the summoning circle.

At the center of the circle stood a beast with graceful wings and a demonic appearance. Its furry hind legs ended in cloven hooves, and its scales were the colors of persimmons. The beast's underbelly, wings, snout, and various markings were a regal purple. Its horns curved slightly, just like in its dog form. It was Socks.

The group stared in awe. He looked both human and not. His leaf-eared, bat-like nose, non-forward-facing eyes, and short tusks made him undeniably otherworldly.

Socks's wingtips had several red smudges. It reminded Koa of the markings on red-bodied swallowtails. Pride demons, which proved to be graceful and stunning, challenged Koa's perception of demons as ugly (demons are why the idiom 'ugly as sin' exists, and for good reason) Socks flared his purple wings with a flourish, holding them high above his head for a moment. His explosive, apocalyptic roar echoed.

Zel opened her soul's eyes. She was in a net of sorts and

floated about. A transparent film covered each net diamond, and the netting itself was an orange-reddish. She could see the parking lot, could see Vih and the others, and felt her essence pouring out fast, like she was a water bucket with several holes. She grew tired by the second.

Oh. I'm in Socks's soul pouch. I guess it makes sense... Zel realized. She heard Sock's thoughts, muddled and fogged by the essence. He wasn't holding to reason.

"Uh... Welcome back..." Koa said. "There's something wrong. He's soul-crazed."

Before Vih could reply, Socks lowered his tail and looked at them. Then he drew Vih's soul from her body. She fell unconscious into Koa's arms as the shiny orb flew into the demon's talons.

Socks tried to drain the magic from Vih's soul, but stopped when a strong taste of bile filled his senses. She hadn't been lying—her soul tasted awful. He gagged, realizing its essence wasn't edible. Socks spat out what he'd taken and released the soul. It was useless to him. But he needed more essence. The pride demon roared and scrambled across the parking lot, jumping across AeroCars and scaring pedestrians.

A gigantic drone flew past the building and hovered above, its four wings making an ear-splitting whirring and blowing wind down on the group. Koa looked up at it.

"Is that the news drone?" Star asked.

"It is," Vih said, getting to her feet with Koa's help.

CHAPTER 34

In another district, in the rescue center, Roxie and Brass slinked past the hodgepodge of stools and chairs, the uneven cobblestones rocking beneath their paws. They halted in an enclosed area bordered by a short white fence ahead. Within, colorful mats and cushions surrounded a colossal TV where familiars and humans alike were engrossed in a movie. Among them sat a vibrant red Chinese crested dog sporting mirrored goggles—Willow. The sight ignited a fury within Roxie, her inner fire simmering, eager to erupt.

"It'll be challenging with just the two of us," Roxie said.

"We planned for three, but we'll manage. She deserves this for imprisoning us," Brass responded, flexing his knuckles.

"We should avenge Socks's feathers," Roxie added, locking eyes with Brass. "Let's exact our revenge." They merged with the grassy surroundings, driven by loyalty to Socks and their own justice. No one tormented their friends without facing consequences, especially not Roxie's.

Willow remained absorbed in the movie, oblivious to the nearing paw steps or faint hissing of forked tongues. As she pondered a distant sound, she found herself airborne, confronted by a keeshond with blazing eyes and bared teeth.

Before Willow could react, Roxie pounced and they collided, tumbling across the grass in a frenzy of tails and claws. Roxie wrestled Willow to the ground, pinning her with relentless force.

In a swift motion, Willow dislodged her goggles, showing her luminous green eyes. The glare caught Roxie off guard, and when she averted her gaze, Willow seized the opportunity to break free, darting off through the crowd, clearing a path with her sharp words and sound horns.

"Oh no..." Brass said, appearing from his hiding spot.

183

Before he and Roxie sprang back into action, the TV turned bright blue, like a spotlight, and shone over them.

"Breaking news," the anchor said. "A clandestine ritual went wrong and summoned a lesser demon to our dimension." The TV showed a girl with wild blonde hair near a rainbow-haired person, someone passed out, plenty of other bystanders, then panned over to a demon in its true form, who swung his enormous tail, annoyed.

"What you are seeing isn't CGI or clever ticks. We have a demon in true form in our dimension. He means no harm... He's just like your familiar, but big. Do not panic."

But Roxie and Brass focused on the demon.

"Is that Socks?" Brass asked. The friends exchanged a glance.

"Go find him. I'll keep tabs on our target and will let you know where she runs off to," Brass said, running off into the ever-growing crowd of people and familiars alike, who couldn't get enough of the news. Roxie watched for a little longer, then bolted off.

CHAPTER 35

Socks rose to his feet. Well, hooves, after taking the souls from a group of young teens nearby, acknowledging the news drone with a wave before adjusting his wings for a better shot. The taste of soul essence lingered, a newfound delight. It filled him with a sense of power, yet beneath it all, guilt gnawed at him. Zel's scream echoed in his mind, a reminder of the pain he'd caused. The teens hadn't been thrilled either, but they were exploring and tickling Sock's throat as they flew around. He couldn't afford to extract too much essence, but knowing Zel was safe, her spirit nestled within his soul pouch, brought a measure of relief. As he gazed at the expanse of the deep blue sky, an irresistible urge to take flight overtook him. Flying was a cherished joy he hadn't indulged in for far too long. Revenge could wait; the open sky beckoned, a rare opportunity he couldn't miss.

Socks, I can't keep the magic up, I am exhausted, he heard Zel's plea.

Too bad... We are going for a little midday flight, his mind spoke back.

What? Socks, no! What if I run out of magic mid-flight? Then what? You will turn into a dog mid-flight and plummet, Zel cried.

Well then. Better keep that magic production up, Socks spat.

He stretched his mighty wings, but something felt awry. Flapping them once, then again, yielded no lift. Attempting to jump and flap only resulted in a thunderous crash as he landed. Frustration roared within Socks and he waved his talons in agitation.

"What's wrong? Can't he fly?" Star asked.

"The square-cube law is hindering him. He lacks

185

enough magic to defy science. Without harsh methods to extract additional essence, he'll revert to his canine form," Vih explained as they approached.

Desperation filled Socks. No, no, no, NO, he thought. I need more magic, NOW.

The souls inside him panicked and flew faster, but the essence production didn't improve.

I... I can't... Please, think of others for once. I'm drained. Show compassion, Socks, Zel's voice echoed in his mind.

If you can't offer enough magic, I'll find more fresh souls, Socks said, activating his demon vision. The cityscape appeared muted, with bright spots representing free souls darting around. His craving to pursue them surged, but none were within reach. A nearby building radiated an intense light akin to a miniature sun. He knew it held many souls. Socks licked his chops in anticipation and headed across a catwalk between buildings, each step draining more of his fading magic.

Hurrying toward the glowing structure, he leaped from one building to another, his movements fluid despite the weight of his demon form.

"What is he doing?" Vih asked as Socks bounded from one skyscraper to the next.

"He's targeting souls. There's a building brimming with them nearby," Star explained.

"Let me guess, demon vision?" Koa asked.

"The wonders of demon vision. That edifice there practically screams 'soul congregation.' I find myself quite intrigued," Star said.

"It's a school. A primary school filled with children under sixteen who haven't attuned yet," Vih said.

CHAPTER 36

From Sock's soul pouch, Zel glimpsed a classroom filled with half-asleep students. A teacher stood before a digital board displaying a hologram of a bright blue, spinning and pixelated triangular bipyramid. The other souls bumped into her, trying to push her off, quite curious themselves.

Their boredom was clear—the students slumped in their seats, their heads propped up by hands, mouths gaping, or resting their heads on the table.

"Does anyone know the formula to calculate the volume of this shape?" the teacher asked, breaking the monotony. Silence, broken only by the teacher's sigh of resignation. Then, her familiar, a little dog with dreadlock-like fur, sauntered in, disrupting the classroom as she sniffed the air, her tail wagging.

"Can you smell that?" the familiar exclaimed. "It's essence, sweet like grape flan. Mm!" The students, unable to smell it, looked up in curiosity, trying to locate the source.

The classroom shook when something crashed onto the roof. Students near the windows spotted a willowy, ketchup-colored tail swinging by. The walls trembled as a hair-raising roar filled the room, prompting everyone to cover their ears. Colorful lights resembling tadpoles emerged from their bodies, rendering them unconscious. The souls streamed toward the open windows and the teacher panicked.

Colorful soul essence rose from the school, converging into Socks's mouth, illuminating his soul pouch like a beacon.

Zel's soul moved, trying to avoid the rapid influx of spirits, and the space got more cramped by the second.

Stop! Socks! Stop this! she pleaded. There was no answer.

"That's one clever demon..." Vih said, noting the

spectacle unfolding before them.

Koa and Star nodded in awe as Socks's hulking figure loomed in the distance.

When the stream of souls ended, Socks closed his mouth, savoring every bit of the sweet essence. Part of him wanted to store the souls forever, to produce as much essence as possible. With a roar, he rose on his hind legs, coiled his tail around the school, spread his wings, and let out another thunderous cry as a lightning bolt streaked across the sky.

Vih wished she could pause time to appreciate the sight before her—Socks wrapped around the building like a cat on a stool, wings spread wide as he prepared to take flight.

With a mighty flap, Socks launched into the air, enjoying the wind beneath his wings and the exhilaration of freedom after so long.

As the pride demon soared between the buildings, his curved talons grazed the smooth windows. It had been too long since he had flown, and he relished every moment. He expected awe and admiration from the humans as he passed the shopping mall's window, but most were too engrossed in their devices to notice.

Only the young children without fancy technology to distract them looked up in wonder as Socks zoomed past, waving back at their excited gestures. A few adults glimpsed of Socks's tail disappearing around a corner.

As he flew higher, Socks's muscles ached, unused to such exertion after years of dormancy. His heart raced, and he panted, his tongue lolling. Despite trying to regain his composure, Socks couldn't suppress the urge to wag his tail, a trait he had observed in the Returned—demons who, as the name implied, had returned to Hell.

Gazing at the city lights below, Socks's smile faded, replaced by a determined expression. He knew he possessed unparalleled power, and with it, the ability to exact revenge on those who had wronged him. His eyes glowed bright purple when he turned his thoughts to Willow. His soul power waned, and Socks knew it was time to focus on his mission. Banking to the left, he started his path, mind set on retribution.

Socks soared over the sprawling city, aiming for the rescue center. He'd get there and finally get his much-needed revenge. He looked to the side. The news drone still followed him. Perhaps he could use it to his benefit. That envy demon had humiliated him in front of the whole rescue center. Willow would learn how much she enjoyed having her fur shaved off in front of the entire Internet, broadcasted to all of Earth, Mars, and Venus. He flew fast.

Socks, Zel called in the back of his mind. *I know what you're planning to do. That is awful, Don't,* Zel said.

She did it to me. She deserves it, and ten times worse, Socks countered.

Exactly, she ripped all your feathers off. How did that feel? Zel asked. She knew doing that was quite cruel of her, and she felt a little bad for it, but she needed to get him to stop before he did something he'd regret.

A burst of purple glow from Socks's eyes and Heart Stone blinded him for a few seconds as if something had exploded next to him. A bitterness so bad his eyes watered and the taste burned his throat and tongue overwhelmed him and he lost control while flying. Plummeting. Once his vision returned, he was coming face-to-face with his ever-enlarging reflection and had to veer sharply to the left to not crash into a rapidly approaching mirrored building. His wingtip grazed the edges as he flew by, eyes wide.

See? It was so dreadful you can't even concentrate when thinking of it. Why do the same thing to someone else? Zel asked in Socks's mind.

One more reason to get revenge, so she knows precisely how it feels. It was wrong, but she did it anyway, Socks thought.

He wanted that envy demon to suffer as much as he had.

Socks, think. Do you really want to cause all that hurt you *suffered to someone else? Would you be happy with yourself if you did so? You think it will bring you closure, but it won't. You will only feel terrible about yourself,* Zel said.

Maybe I could let go... My feathers will grow back, Socks thought. *But so will her fur.* His mind shot back. She deserved it.

Socks... Please, have some compassion.

I'll think about it, Socks thought to shut Zel up. He had no intention of considering it, but he hoped she'd stop annoying him as he beelined across the cityscape.

A bright shiny silver speck appeared in the distance, past the buildings. It approached quickly, growing, a silver-like arrow. It was on a crash course with Socks.

The demon tried veering right. The speck did the same. Socks feared it was a missile targeting him. He wasn't causing any destruction. When he flew past, people were not running, but staring in awe, so they did not experience fear. At least it didn't look it.

Socks's fear of the military faded when the speck got close enough. It was an AeroCar. Once near, it stopped and hovered in front of Socks. Roxie, Socks's best friend, sat in the familiar basket.

"Socks, oh my. Are those souls? Where did you get all those?" Roxie asked, magnifying her voice over the vehicle's speakers.

"At a school," Socks said.

"Hm." She scratched her chin. Not exactly the answer she expected. "Hey. Are you heading to the rescue center for revenge?"

Socks nodded.

"The envy demon ran off. But Brass is tracking her down. I'm tracking his location. Find him, and we find her. Follow me."

Socks, wait, no. Please don't hurt anyone, Zel begged.

I *won't. I'll just give someone a grisly haircut. And I won't have your disapproving stare following me every step of the way.*

Socks spit out Zel's bright, multicolored soul into one of his gigantic talons before she had time to reply.

"I'll see you later," he said, releasing the soul. He didn't want her to be judgy and pour her disapproving thoughts directly into his mind as he exacted revenge. He had so much soul essence, one soul less didn't matter. It flew up, then shot back in the direction it had come from, dashing back to Zel's body. Socks turned to Roxie.

Roxie turned around the AeroCar and turned left. Socks followed with intense wing beats.

Back in the skyscraper's parking lot, Koa paced as Vih stood there. "I don't even know what is happening anymore," they said, throwing up their hands in frustration.

"What is that?" Star asked, pointing at a speck in the sky. A colorful bead appeared, like a brand-new star. It shot toward Zel's body, then dove into her rib cage, as if it was diving into a pool.

Zel's eyes popped open, and she gasped, springing up, then lost her balance from the sudden position change. Koa rushed to her and caught her before she face-planted.

"What's happening?" they asked, helping their friend up.

"I'll explain on the way," Zel said. "We need to find Socks and convince him to not follow through with his revenge plans."

"Woah, calm down. Revenge on whom?" Star asked.

"Long story. Now let's go!" Zel opened the AeroCar's door and jumped in.

Socks trailed Roxie's AeroCar, wings beating hard as they neared the shore. The salty sea breeze ruffled his leg fur, and the rhythmic crashing of waves filled the air. Roxie led him to a stretch of beach where a lighthouse stood, many people milling about.

"She's there somewhere," Roxie shouted from the AeroCar. "I'll park and meet you."

Socks nodded and folded his wings, diving and landing lightly on the wet sand. Seashells crunched beneath his hooves as he scanned the area. Some people fled screaming. Others lowered their sunglasses, gasped, and went "Eh, just another demon" before going back to relaxing. The lighthouse loomed above him, and people appeared on a balcony on the side to stare down at him. Had Willow hidden there?

As he thought, a loud noise startled him, and pain shot through his left wing membrane. A small arrow made from a broken tree branch, with razors for the fletching, embedded itself in the sand. Socks picked it up with a talon. The point was very sharp. A skittering caught his attention, and a flash of red fur darted across the sand. Willow. She raced toward the rocky shoreline, her paws kicking up sand.

"Very clever..." he said, trying to move his wing, but pain prevented him from doing so. "Now I can't fly without tearing it more. Your kind can never be miserable alone, can you? If you can't fly, you'll be sure that no one else can!"

Socks ran, giving Willow chase as she navigated the slippery rocks. She yipped and shot into a tide pool, trying to hide beneath the surface.

Socks hesitated before the seaweed-covered rocks. Ocean spray cooled his scales. Hooves weren't that great on slippery surfaces. He peered into the pool, but Willow was nowhere in sight. The water distorted her form, and he couldn't reach her with his talons. Frustrated, Socks slammed his tail against the water, sending a spray of seawater into the air.

Willow surfaced, gasping for breath, and swam

toward the open sea. Socks snarled and leaped into the ocean after her. The cold water closed around him, and he propelled himself through the waves with his powerful limbs. His talons nearly grazed her tail, but Willow was fast, darting through the water like a fish.

It makes sense Willow matched to Zel... They both share unmet needs and a love for swimming, he thought.

Willow swam toward a cluster of sharp rocks that jutted out of the sea like shark teeth. Socks hesitated—those rocks could tear him apart if he wasn't careful. It was already too deep. He worried he'd have trouble making it back to the distant shore. But Willow had no such concern as she headed for the rocks.

Zel's AeroCar flew over the sandy stretch.

"I see them! On the sea!" Zel pointed to an obvious demon swimming. Then the AeroCar halted midair and refused to go further.

"What's wrong? ADAN, get us to those rocks," Zel said.

"Sorry. The area is too crowded, and AeroCars are forbidden. I can scan for the nearest parking space," ADAN said.

"I knew we should have kept you disabled, you pile of code," Koa muttered.

"There is no time! ADAN, drop me off!" Zel said.

"Sure thing," the AI said, and made a brief stop at a drop off point next to the sand. Zel jumped out, taking off her shoes and socks and ran toward the sea, dropping her jacket and any other unnecessary items as she went. She dashed to the sea, jumped into the cold water, and dolphin kicked her way to the sharp rocks. She had to reach Socks before he reached Willow.

Cursing under his breath, Socks hauled himself out of the water onto a nearby boulder to rest. His hind legs kept

193

slipping off, his hooves had no traction. He watched the waves crash against the rocks, searching for any sign of the Chinese crested dog. A red flash climbed onto one of the jagged rocks. He jumped into the sea again. Willow saw him and tried to swim away. But Socks grabbed her and hoisted her back onto the rock.

Socks loomed over the soaked dog... Or tried to. It was very hard to loom when you can't stand upright because the surface is too slippery.

"Gotcha," Socks said.

"Wait! I'm sorry, alright? I am so sorry! Please! Have mercy!" Willow begged, looking at the blue vastness and rocky edges surrounding them.

"Begging didn't help me. Why do you think it will help you?" Socks asked and stared down at the dog in front of him. Into her bright green eyes.

She trembled in fear...Or was it cold? Because it was cold. He decided it was fear. Just what he'd hoped would happen—that Willow would realize she had picked on the worst possible familiar, and would shiver under his might. But... something was wrong. Socks didn't feel as much satisfaction as he thought he would. He felt... pity. That was the word.

He remembered Zel.

"Try to think of others," she had said. Zel had told him to have compassion. Which he considered being a bunch of nonsense. Why was he thinking about it when he was so close to getting his revenge? Willow didn't deserve his—or anyone's—compassion, despite what Zel thought. He stepped forward, ready to exact revenge, but looking at that trembling dog lit something deep within his non-soul.

Socks was orders of magnitude more powerful than the demon... But he had been as scared as she was. He had begged for mercy like she was doing, and the fact they had

194

denied it was simply horrible. Maybe Zel was right. Maybe he didn't feel like inflicting so much hurt on others when they looked as desperate and as frightened as he did, and when he knew the exact depth of the consequences.

Socks seethed. *She deserves to suffer for what she did.* Willow's raised hackles and trembling form triggered a painful memory he'd long buried.

Back in Hell, Socks had once trembled, too. In a cramped bedroom, he had stood over the shattered remains of a mug decorated with galloping horses. His sketch pad, depicting the room, felt heavy in his hands. When he had turned to sketch the curtains, his tail had knocked the mug off the table. He considered trying to glue it back together.

Hoofbeats echoed through the stone hallways. Socks's heart pounded. He considered escape, but the window was too close to the door to reach. He ducked into the closet, peering through the gap, just as a demon, draped in flowing silk over his horns and with shiny leaf-green scales, entered. Oh no... wrath demon, Socks thought, dread settling in his stomach.

The greater demon noticed the broken mug and erupted in fury, spewing bright red flames. The closet heated uncomfortably. Socks shielded his eyes with his wings, fighting the urge to leap out.

"Who broke this?" the demon roared, stomping around. "I know you're here. It will be worse if I find you."

The closet doors flew open. Blinding light stunned Socks and thick talons wrapped around his arm, yanking him out.

"Look at what you did!" the wrath demon shouted. "I know you did it. Look!"

"I didn't—"

"Do you think I'm blind?"

"It was an accident. I'm sorry," Socks pleaded.

The demon's grip tightened. "That mug was

SPECIAL!" she yelled, then hurled Socks through the window. Glass shards sliced his scales and wing membranes. He tried to fly, but a crushing weight made him crash to the ground.

"You're not leaving before getting punished," the wrath demon shouted, her hot breath searing his back. "This is so you don't run off again."

There was a snap and screamed and searing pain shot through Socks's right wing.

All Socks had wanted that day was a bit of understanding that accidents happened, and he hadn't done it under any ill will. All he wanted was for someone to pat him on the back, maybe say he could buy another one, and explain why that one was special. He already felt bad enough for breaking it. The ones he had opened to had been pretty apathetic to it, and said, 'at least it smarted you.' Socks didn't think it did.

Looking at Willow, cornered and trembling, teeth out, reminded him of himself that day. She'd done something wrong, knew it, but had hoped there would be no consequences.

But Willow deserves it. She did it on purpose. There should be consequences. But Zel would hate it if I did it... Which doesn't matter. Or maybe it does, Socks thought. He imagined getting revenge and strutting back to Zel, only for his behavior to horrify and disgust her.

Socks splashed sea water on them both with his tail. Willow cowered even more. Zel only disagreed with him because of her bond with Willow. Or maybe she thought his actions were exaggerated, like the wrath demon's had been. The wrath demon was a returned; that mug was probably the only thing she had brought back. Since Socks understood human friendships better, he saw why she was outraged. But he still thought she was wrong for throwing him out the window and disciplining him further.

He didn't want to lose his friendship with Zel, but he didn't want to forgive Willow, either. She'd caused a permanent emotional scar. His feathers would grow back, but his memory wouldn't fade. In Hell, mistakes always fly back into your face, no matter how old they are.

Socks wanted her to suffer even more. If it were anyone else, Zel wouldn't care as much. But she saw herself in Willow. Which said a lot about her distorted self-image, because they were nothing alike.

But Zel doesn't need me to forgive. She understands me. She just doesn't want me to do the same dreadful thing. Is Zel right? Would I never forgive myself if I did it? But she deserves it... Willow hurt me. I should get payback. But... She looks so scared. Maybe being chased around the city is already punishment enough.

"Why did you do it?" Socks spat.

"What?" Willow stuttered.

"My feathers. Why?" Socks growled. Willow sat in silence. "Answer me," he snarled, then roared for emphasis. She ducked, her eyes shining green.

"I... got paid to do it. Not in money. I was promised a match with the right person. Some diligent angel paid me. I don't know his name," she said.

Harper. Has to be, Socks thought. *He must have been trying to shame me into returning to Hell.*

"But you deserved it. You don't remember it, your kind never does, but you were mean to me. You trounced over all my feelings. You thought you were so much better than everyone else because of those stupid feathers of yours," Willow said.

Socks roared in frustration. He should make Willow suffer and hide in embarrassment forever. But maybe... he could let go. Not forgive—that wouldn't happen. His feathers would grow back. Maybe Zel was right, and maybe not seeking revenge was for the best.

I hope I don't regret not doing it

That meant he didn't need the souls anymore. Socks raised on his legs, and one by one, he let the souls go. A bright light shone from his soul pouch. Socks felt his true form grow less stable as the magic poured out. His wings dissolved, starting from the very tips, akin to glitter blowing away on a windy day.

"What are you doing?" Willow whispered in awe.

"Giving up this power before I stop being in a merciful mood," Socks said, walking in circles. Magic emanated from his wings, fading into a glittery mist of several colors in the sky. Socks's demonic build became less defined. It blurred, like a creature seen in a dream. With each circle, more light enveloped him 'til it engulfed him.

Not that far away, an AeroCar with turtle graffiti on it sped through the beach looking for a parking spot as Vih looked for any signs of a giant demon flying about.

"What's that?" Vih asked in wonder, pointing as lights of every single color spread out, coming from a rocky cliff in the sea. It looked like an aurora. The colorful light swayed and danced in the air, spreading out and soaring. A barrage of souls followed soon after, heading in the same direction, like a school of fish.

"That's soul essence. My dear Socks must've unleashed the souls. I can't believe he's wasting such fine morsels," Star said.

On the sea, a surge of emotion flooded Zel as the souls flew over her. She raised a trembling hand to her mouth. Tears rolled down her cheeks, and a smile curled on her lips. "He didn't hurt her," she whispered, watching the colorful barrage and savoring the relief, before continuing to the sharp rocks.

As the magic faded and spread, Socks shrank even more. His talons became paws, and his hooves morphed into claws. Long ears with flowy hair sprouted from his head, unfurling with grace. His tusks shrunk till they were nothing but cone-shaped teeth. Fur sprouted all over. The yellow light flared, then faded, like a lightbulb burning out. Where a massive hulking beast had stood laid an English toy spaniel, all curled up.

Socks got up and shook himself. He looked at his paws, then walked in a circle, trying to eye his back. He'd barely returned and already missed his wings. His strength. And everything. But that was the price of staying. Giving all of that up. He hoped he wouldn't regret it later. But that was enough pouting. He had more pressing matters. Socks eyed Willow, who was still cowering, trembling, despite the defiant look in her eyes. Socks didn't know what to expect. But he still felt empty. It hadn't helped. He just had given up a load of power. He still felt hurt and needed closure. If Zel's way didn't work...

"I can't forgive you. I don't think I ever will ... And I changed my mind about having mercy. You'd look better as a furless variant," Socks said and stepped forward.

Willow was about to jump into the sea again when a rogue wave towered over the rock they were on, ready to crash.

Socks jumped and dove into the wave. Willow tried to do the same, but she missed the timing. The monster wave crashed on her. Socks watched underwater as the wave flung Willow into a rock. Demon's horns weren't decoration, they could handle quite an impact, and that's what saved her life. She crashed horns first, putting the strain on the thickest part of her skull, but she was rendered unconscious, and sank.

Socks dove after her, toward the ever-darkening water. He didn't have it in him to let her die. But he wasn't that good of a swimmer either.

Strong hands wrapped around his ribcage and pulled him to the surface at an incredible speed. He filled his lungs with air, but still gasped.

"What are... you doing!" Socks said, panting, kicking to be let go.

"Saving you from drowning!" It was Zel.

"I'm not! Willow is! S—" Before he could finish his sentence, Zel let him go and disappeared. He looked around at the sea. For a moment, he was alone, and it was scary. Then Zel broke the surface, bringing Willow back from the depths.

The envy demon's eyes fluttered open a few seconds later, and she gasped and took in deep breaths. She looked at Socks, then at Zel, but said nothing.

"Smartwatch, get me a rescue drone!" Zel ordered.

Her smartwatch chimed. Socks watched a device take off from the shore and fly toward them.

CHAPTER 37

It wasn't long before Socks was back on the sand. Willow was a bit away, first aid robots checking her over. From what he could see, she seemed fine. His desire to shave her was gone. But he couldn't place why. He was still empty... but he doubted revenge would fill the gap.

Socks watched the envy demon, his eyelids heavy and drooping until his eyes closed. He opened his eyes wide, to not let it happen again. Thought it felt like a bag of sand sat on him, the exhaustion making his legs shake. Socks glanced around, wishing for a soft place to rest. Fatigue took him. His legs refused to work and his eyes shut as he collapsed.

"Got you," Zel said, catching Socks before he crashed hard onto the sand. She helped him back to his feet.

"Mrrp..." he said. He planned on saying thanks, but it didn't work. He yawned, and he tried again.

"Are you alright?" Zel kneeled beside Socks, her hand gently caressing his soft fur.

Socks nodded. "But I am exhausted—" Socks began, his words cutting off when he expelled a gooey, cyan substance onto the sand. Zel recoiled in alarm as Socks attempted to clean his mouth with a paw, only for more goo to emerge moments later.

"Is that blood? Is he alright?" Zel turned to the vet student, her concern clear.

"Demon blood sizzles. It's soul essence," Star explained.

"Did he eat too much?" Zel asked. Socks continued to expel the strange substance.

"No, but soul essence can be quite potent. Think of how humans born on Mars struggle with Earth's gravity; it's a similar concept," Star said.

Everything is spinning, Socks communicated

telepathically. Zel offered him a sympathetic glance as Koa approached, pinching a round, crimson pastille in their fingers.

"Here, you don't deserve this, but it will make you feel better," Koa offered, prompting Socks to accept the pastille.

He took it. It was dry and grainy, like sand, and crumbled in his mouth. A metallic and greasy taste overwhelmed his senses.

"I know it tastes horrible. Trust me, you'll feel better," Koa reassured.

After a few tense moments, Socks relaxed. "Better?" they asked.

Yes, much better, Socks relayed through his telepathic connection to Zel.

"He says yes and thanks," Zel translated, relieved Socks was finding some relief.

He stood up.

Zel waited a few seconds to be sure he was fine, then got up and paced. "Never, ever do that again, you hear me? It was terrifying! I know my soul's essence will replenish, but it felt awful. And you used it for something awful! No draining essence like that ever again! For a moment, I was afraid you'd toss me into a volcano or stab me with a pitchfork just to get more. Never act that scary and vengeful again." Zel's voice trembled with anger as she locked eyes with him. Her pupils dilated and her nostrils flared.

Socks could only stare, stunned. He hadn't realized Zel could become that furious.

She clenched her fists; her face flushed with frustration. "And then you went to that school! I can't believe it! I was too shocked to even speak. How could you do that? You traumatized an entire busload of kids! I was afraid you'd hurt them, hurt me. Never pull something like that again! And it hurt when you bit my soul. A lot," Zel continued.

Her thoughts were a jumble of conflicting emotions

Socks couldn't decipher into coherent words or images.

Zel kneeled before him, her gaze intense. "Never again, understood?" she demanded, her voice brimming with even more intensity and her head moved closer to his.

He nodded, and she hugged him. "Hey, I'm glad you didn't get your revenge. It must have been hard to let her go. I can tell something changed in you," Zel said, petting him.

Socks wagged his tail. Pets felt good... even though he still didn't fancy being a lapdog. *There is a change in you too...* Socks said via telepathy. There were muffled, sandy footsteps. Socks looked behind him.

Roxie and Brass approached, both with their mouths open in surprise.

"Socks, you had her at your mercy... And you did nothing. Why?" Brass asked.

Socks glanced at his paws. He wasn't sure. Maybe because she was too scared. Maybe because he saw himself in her. Or maybe Zel was right. But he didn't have time to answer.

"I CAN'T BELIEVE WE DID ALL THIS WORK. AFTER WHAT SHE DID, YOU JUST LET HER GO? THAT'S JUST SO... SO... SO..." Roxie growled, then her fur ignited into bright red flames. Brass stepped to the side. Her fire crackled, burned, and almost turned purple. She breathed hellfire into the sky, causing everyone to duck and look for cover.

"She's blinded by rage. Hide, she won't care who she unleashes her anger on, even if isn't the right person," Koa said and ran behind a robot selling ice cream. Zel bolted, carrying Socks with her. Star followed Koa, and Vih was nowhere to be seen.

Roxie's fire was so bright those at the tops of the nearest skyscrapers could see it. She raged more, yelling mean things, stomping her feet, and insulting everybody. Then, her fire shone like a star, and exploded like a supernova. Zel waited a little longer before daring to peek from her hiding place. When she did, all that remained was the keeshond on the sizzling sand lying down, panting, all the glow from her eyes gone.

Socks scurried from Zel's lap and rushed to his friend. Brass approached too. Both helped Roxie up.

"So... are you feeling better now?" Brass asked.

"I am. I needed that. Although..." Roxie started, then her eyes lit in flames again. "How could you? I'm still mad," she snapped at Socks, who shied away.

"Hey, Zel. These are my friends Roxie and Brass."

"Oh. Hello... Roxie and Brass," Zel said, greeting the two. They were unimpressed.

"It's the other way round," Brass said.

Roxie nodded, puffing sparks of irritation from her nose.

Koa, Vih and Star came out of their hiding places, too.

"So, about that unattuning ritual. When are we going to try that again?" Socks asked, earning a look from everyone.

"Never," Koa said.

"Try getting used to essence first," said Star.

"I think we're getting along. How about we try staying together longer?" Zel asked.

"But what about your sea expedition thing?" Socks asked. Zel gave him a sad look and explained.

CHAPTER 38

In the dusky evening, within the confines of Harper's bedroom at the rescue center, tension hung in the air. Harper paced, his talons clicking against the cold floor. Souls writhed and screamed in a boiling pot nearby, another been tied down to a chopping board tried to wriggle free. A menacing meat tenderizer sat next to it.

Meanwhile, Rubicallophrys, cocooned in blankets upon the bed, faked calm.

"I'm so glad we rescued you... But it worries me you said things. What did you tell them?" Harper asked.

"Some things... not important things," he said.

"You'll have to be more specific there," Harper pressed.

His friend sighed, then opened up.

"Are you sure Socks didn't lie?" Harper's frustration bubbled up, his beak clacking with irritation. He approached the table near the stove and grabbed the tenderizer with a talon. The soul wriggled even more.

"He wouldn't deceive his best friend. If you misplaced the recipe in one of those magazines, it's likely lost," Rubicallophrys said.

"I'm more worried that we can't frame him like we planned. I was so careful to hide every piece of evidence subtly so he wouldn't notice, but now..." Harper raised the hammer.

"There's always the backup plan. Speaking of which, read my report. Castan's connections came in handy. Plenty we can use," Rubicallophrys suggested.

Harper's expression didn't seem pleased. "We're running out of time! We need that recipe, or everything falls apart!" he stressed.

Rubicallophrys was about to respond when new arrivals interrupted them. Harper turned to two ravens, adorned with helmets bearing Abundance's insignia, bowing to him.

"I hope it's good news," Harper muttered, sensing the tension and placing the hammer down for the moment.

"Something's happening on the Internet," one of the soldiers began.

"You'll have to be more specific," Harper prompted.

"Videos of Dryas in dog form, attuned to a human, one with rainbow hair. They even put their coat on him, likely to shield him from the stares. The videos are going viral, along with multiple eyewitness accounts at the smuggler's market," the soldier explained.

Harper shot Rubicallophrys a pointed look.

"I wouldn't do something that reckless," Rubicallophrys said.

"The videos must have been AI. Please tell me you dispelled the rumors," Harper demanded.

"We tried, as did others, but there were too many witnesses. One, Hawke, saw him up close and was convinced. She's offered to show us," the soldier said.

"Hawke? The infamous greed demon?" Harper exclaimed.

"Yes. She also has no business being a raven," the other soldier confirmed.

"He couldn't have been the real one. You fell for a hoax. I bet she charged a hefty price for her 'insight,'" Harper accused, noting the soldiers' guilty expressions.

"It wasn't a hoax. Dryas had a scar over his heart. We witnessed him manipulating essence. But something was off. He seemed disoriented," the soldier admitted.

"How so?" Harper asked.

"He was surprised Abundance still stood, and, strangest of all, he asked who ruled it!" the soldier said.

Harper and Rubicallophrys exchanged

a glance in silence.

"Do you have any... samples of the essence he manipulated?" Harper asked.

The soldiers nodded and handed him a glowing, floating orb of light.

Harper pecked it tentatively. The essence flowed into his mouth. It tasted both sweet and sour. Like the sauce. Its unusual richness provided him with a boost of energy, enhancing his senses. He felt more awake. He could think better. Fight better. It was like a fogginess had clouded his mind and senses, but it had vanished.

"Only Dryas can collect the essence that rich... It is him," Harper muttered. His eyes gleamed with malevolent glee. "This means we aren't lost. We can still rise above the humans. We can end our starvation. All we need is to make Dryas teach us his secret. Then, we'll be saved. Humanity will return to where it belongs—under our feet"

Harper grinned at his friend, his mind swirling with fantasies of glory. They would build statues in his honor. Demons would learn of him, how he never stopped fighting, how he refused to let humans starve them, how Harper saved them all.

CHAPTER 39

Castan, the actual Castan, sat near his colleagues as their boss paced, scolding them. He reached into his pocket for a flavorless candy made for pride demons to rid them of bitterness without being sugary. He found only empty packets.

The shapeshifter had spilled info on everyone. Though the demons had tried to get the imposter to talk about himself, they appreciated his crack down on Castan's teamwork.

"The only reason you're getting away with just a scolding is because the mission didn't exist. Castan, you're reassigned to work under Chili because at least she follows the books! You weren't following anything, doing whatever you wanted, and your colleagues covered for you! Don't give me that 'we showed results' excuse. Your team has shown nothing but failure. If I knew you'd shirk your team leader duties, I'd never have made you one! Now get out before I decide I've been too light on you."

The three of them hurried into the corridor, walking together as always. Chili's tail swished anxiously. Before, she wasn't officially a team leader. She couldn't shove Castan's duties back to him. Chili had to handle them herself, without his help, and it scared her. They had reassigned her, for real.

"Chili, you'll do fine," Castan said, guessing her thoughts. "I'm not leaving."

"I think you'll be great no matter what mission we get next," Spark agreed.

Chili wasn't so sure. All she could think of was the graph and how they only succeeded because the shapeshifter led them, not her. She felt like a weak leader.

"I hope so... Now, let's get ice cream to cope with all that talking," Chili said.

CHAPTER 40

A few days later, Zel strolled down the lobby of the rescue center, her gaze drawn to the vibrant tiles adorning the walls. Each hue seemed to whisper tales of the demons that had found refuge within the walls.

Following the drone, Zel stood before a door to a bedroom, anticipation bubbling within her chest. She pressed the doorbell, only to be met with silence.

"My system says she's inside," the drone said.

"Hello, Willow? Are you there? It's Zel," she said.

As if summoned by her words, nails clicked on the floor from the other side, and Zel's jaw nearly dropped—a hairless dog adorned in an oversized sweater and ski goggles peered out through the dog door, a curious blend of emotions in its gaze.

Willow's once luxurious silky coat from her head to tail was missing, and Willow stood before her, stripped bare of her fur. Though Zel knew the reason behind Willow's unusual appearance, it was best if she mentioned nothing of it.

"Hello. I felt like I should come here and say... That..."

Zel didn't know what to say. She wasn't at a loss for words. In fact, her problem was the exact opposite. She had way too many words she wanted to say and didn't know how to translate all those thoughts into speech. Saying 'I think you're cruel and mean and never want to see you again,' probably wasn't the way to go.

"You are exchanging me for someone else," Willow said.

"It's not about replacing you, Willow. I... I just couldn't break the bond with Socks, and I don't know if I ever will."

"I understand," she murmured and retreated to the safety of her room.

Once Zel reached the lobby, her gaze fell upon Socks,

talking to both Roxie and Brass, and all three seemed thrilled. Socks didn't look sorry to learn his friends had shaved someone. She understood his slight comfort in it. He probably felt the world was a little less unfair.

Zel approached them. Socks gave Roxie and Brass one hug each, and said they should keep in touch, then walked to Zel's side and the two headed to the door.

"You look smug," Zel said playfully.

"She deserved it. And they used clippers to do it. It's not like it hurt, unlike having your feathers plucked. That really hurt," Socks said.

Zel rolled her eyes, some warmth for him blossoming in her heart. "Koa gave me the contact for several places that focus on sea life and accept volunteers," Zel said.

"Which ones did you apply for?" Socks asked.

"Every single one of them. Besides, I'm now looking for a better part-time job. Mom is right. Time to start plan B... Alright. Let's go. We don't want to keep the others waiting at the aquarium."

CHAPTER 41

Vibrant ecosystems thrived under the gentle blue glow of submerged lights within the aquarium's depths. Knobby coral and delicate sea sponges cast ethereal shadows against the glass, their intricate forms reminiscent of ancient sculptures carved by vast stretches of time. Zel's gaze wandered, mesmerized by the otherworldly beauty surrounding her.

Among the coral formations, various shapes danced in the currents—a diversity of life that inhabited the waters. Upside-down horn-like structures protruded from the sandy substrate, their tops adorned with colorful anemone-like things that swayed in the gentle rhythm of the waves: a rugose coral. Massive gray fish glided gracefully through the water, their sleek forms weaving between clusters of sea turtles with elegantly elongated tails. Resting on the pale sand below were massive moray eels.

Zel settled into a cushioned chair, her eyes on the underwater world before her. A shy octopus emerged from its hiding place, its cleverly disguised form blending seamlessly into the surrounding reef—a master of camouflage in its underwater realm.

Conversation ebbed and flowed among her companions, and Vih went on in depth about the ecology of the sights before them. Star was the only one who still paid attention to her rambling, admiration bright, his eyes alight with wonder at the barrage of information about the coral formations.

"So, let's see if I understood, you paid a whole ninety rias to see, not the sharks, not the eels, the seahorses, all those deep-sea fish, or those big squids, but to stare at that blob spiked into the floor?" Koa asked, arms folded.

"I think they look cute," Star said.

"I wonder if that's how rugose corals looked back then. We tried our very best with this one. It turned out so pretty," Zel said in awe. One day, she'd work on genetics and help bring back extinct species and make new ones. It was her dream. They were in the aquarium's cafeteria. People, service robots, and familiars mingled in a cacophony of noise.

"We are on TV," Vih said, and the group directed their gaze to the wall-sized TV on the other side of the room. It featured coverage of their ill ritual attempts. Zel paired her smartwatch to the tv, and once connected, the sound transmitted to her earphones.

"A clandestine ritual summoned a lesser demon into our dimension," the anchor reported, accompanied by footage of Socks in his true form darting about the city.

"While initially appearing agitated, the demon soon acclimated to its surroundings. Concerns arose regarding the souls it took along the way, but researchers assure us all souls were returned before the demon departed. Many worried if the souls were harmed, so let's hear what they have to say," the anchor continued, segueing into an interview with a young girl with a ponytail.

"It was incredible! I got to see the whole city. I was exhausted, but it was totally worth it," the girl exclaimed, responding to the reporter's questions about her experience.

"No, it didn't hurt," she added.

The segment then shifted to a dark-skinned boy of the same age.

"I thought it was awesome! Whoever that was saved me from a boring class. And no, I didn't feel a thing," the boy chimed in.

"Ignorance is bliss," Koa said, eliciting a surge of indignation from Socks.

"What makes you think I'd harm a bunch of

children?" Socks said.

"A hunch," Koa said with a sly grin, though Socks failed to find the humor in it.

"Anyway, Star, there's something I've been wanting to ask. Can you explain what this is and why Harper's turning Hell upside down to find it?" Socks asked.

He then eyed Zel, who took a moment to understand he wanted the magazine. She handed it to him, and he handed it to Star.

It smelled of sulfur and had a nice skyline on the cover page.

"I bookmarked it for you," Socks said.

Star flipped the pages until he reached one scribbled in black ink. His writing. Number, formulas, and methods. But it was incomplete. Half-written. The recipe Harper had been looking for.

"No idea what this is. I've never seen this sheet music in my life," Star countered, a hint of defensiveness in his tone.

"You lived in Abundance, your accent is a hint, and I believe this is your handwriting, not a sheet music, Dryas," Socks said, not backing down.

"It's not my handwriting! Mine is way worse than this! Everyone always complained they couldn't read my signature or certain notes and—" Star stopped when he realized Socks was giving him the smuggest look, but he didn't know why. Then it dawned on him Socks had called him Dryas and he had answered.

"Ah! No! It was... I... Didn't pay attention to what you said! I just..."

"Everyone knows it is you, Dryas. No need to pretend you're not you," Socks said.

Zel gave him a look.

"I can't believe you're alive. That's why you insisted Dryas isn't a shapeshifter so much... And why you got so mad when I mentioned your poor financial judgment," Socks said, the pieces falling into place.

"Poor financial judgment? Quite the contrary! It was a stroke of visionary brilliance," Star said, giving up hopes of hiding his identity any longer.

Star stared at the page. It was part of his method for extracting soul essence. He had tried to write the secret and tell Harper how to extract the richest essence from souls. It would end the famine, restore their power, strengthen the shields, and keep the Abominations at bay. But Harper was... harsh. Very harsh. Star recalled the atrocities Harper had committed against his peers, the ruthless cruelty of his definition of 'disciplining.' What horrors would he unleash on human souls, beings he saw as beneath him?

That was why Star had never shared his knowledge. He sensed Harper's ambitions stretched far beyond a contented city of well-fed angels. But what did he truly want? Whatever it was, it couldn't be good.

It isn't fair to the souls... Harper will torture them beyond measure, Star thought, a chill running down his spine. *But if I don't help, the starvation will only worsen.*

"Have I told you I deeply dislike this oily speech of yours and I want to beat it out of you?" Socks asked, drawing Star's attention from the magazine.

"Oily? Ha, ha. I am genuine, dear. I don't say things to please my colleagues. I say what's on my mind," Star said.

Socks didn't look convinced.

"Koa's sealing ritual saved your life, didn't it?" Zel asked the blue dog.

"Star! Why didn't you—Why... That explains some... Why didn't you tell me sooner that you're this demon king thing?" Koa said.

"More like an angel king," Socks teased.

Star paled. "People tend to get a little... angry, when

learning these things. Like torches and pitchforks sort of angry..." Star attempted to explain.

"To be fair, Star, I knew it. I figured it out when we were drinking tea, and you acted... odd. But I was hoping you'd tell us yourself," Zel said.

"Same," Vih said.

"Wait, so all of you already knew? Am I the only one who didn't? What... Star! You should have trusted me!" Koa said.

"So you could make sure to put a stake through my heart again?" Star asked.

"Sheesh. You're not a vampire, you know?" Koa said.

"That kills more than vampires... Wait... did you say 'again'?" Did you put a stake through his heart?" Vih asked.

"No! I'm not sure what he's talking about. It was an accident, wasn't me, and it wasn't a stake!" Koa said.

"Now, about that writing..." Socks pressed.

Star sighed. "Harper had been begging me to share my knowledge. One night I begrudgingly started this, but I never finished because I didn't want to give it to him. When he asked me how things were going, I lied. I said I wrote it down, and shortly after I became stranded in the human realm. The city still standing without me ruling it surprises me. I need to go back to Abundance. Something odd is going on there. I can tell. Someone there might know something. I need to do something for my city, my subjects! I can't leave them in Harper's hands!" Star said.

ABOUT THE AUTHOR

Sage Lockwood, an author and illustrator, is passionate about weaving stories that spark the imagination. Currently visiting her family in Paraguay, she shares her room—and her creativity—with her beloved pet rabbit, Bunny.

www.ingramcontent.com/pod-product-compliance
Lightning Source LLC
Chambersburg PA
CBHW020642260626
47157CB00008B/2874